West Virginia Ghos

Copyright © 2017 by J

West Virginia Ghost Stories, Legends, and ...

ISBN-13: 978-1-940087-25-2

21 Crows Dusk to Dawn Publishing, 21 Crows, LLC

All rights reserved. No part of this book may be reproduced or transmitted in any form or by any means, electronic or
mechanical, including photocopying, recording, or by any information storage and retrieval system, without permission in writing from the copyright owner.

This is a work of fiction. Names, characters, places and incidents either are the product of the author's imagination or are used fictitiously, and any resemblance to any actual persons, living or dead, events, or locales is entirely coincidental. This book was printed in the United States of America.

Disclaimer: Yes, I went to all these places. I've been to over 900—and still counting. Probably a lot more. I don't like to count because then I feel like it's becomes a competition. It's not. I just like finding old places that have ghost stories attached to them. I try to find places my readers can visit. If they can't visit, they might be able to drive past and get a feel for the history and the ghost associated with it. Or maybe just read about the old legends nearby.

Most of the time, I'm dragging my kids with me. I've found if I offer them some great shops to visit like True Treats Historic Candy in Harpers Ferry or find them adventures like Hatfield McCoy Airboat Rides in Matewan, they like coming along. But mostly, we all like to listen to the ghost stories—Chuck Ghent, tour guide, told us a bunch from Moundsville Prison—and we get to know a lot of people with colorful characters. A few have even taken us on their own adventures.

The stories and legends in this book are for enjoyment purposes and taken from many different resources. Many have been passed down and have been altered along the way. I attempt to sort through the many different variations found on a story and find the most popular and the most supported by historical evidence. Not all sources and legends can be substantiated. I try to give you the basic research and history so you can delve into the stories, enjoy them, discover something.

I probably don't need to tell you this, but I will anyway: anyone exploring ghosts should always respect the areas to search out the paranormal and also respect those who are still living who might be related to the dead. Public properties may become private after the printing of the book or they may simply be listed with the address so you know the historical area where the story originated. Regardless if the area is listed as private or not, please respect the landowner and do not disturb their privacy. Listing the GPS and address does not imply you are welcome to visit, nor that you visit without contacting the property owner. It is to give you a visual of the location where the haunting occurred. Call ahead of time to make sure you are not trespassing. Ghost hunting can be a dangerous endeavor due to the many different environmental factors including many that are done in the darkness, forests, in old buildings or in hazardous areas. Before visiting any haunted site, verify location, accessibility and safety. I never recommend venturing into unknown areas in darkness or entering private or public property without prior permission or parking in the darkness to see if a car rolls uphill. Don't go into train tunnels if the railroad is still in use. GPS routes may change or become hazardous. Always check with owners/operators of public and private areas to see if a license is needed to hunt and to check for unsafe areas. Make sure you follow all laws and abide by the rules of any private or public region you use. Readers assume full responsibility for use of information in this book. Please use common sense.

Table of Contents—West Virginia Ghost/Legends

Northwestern West Virginia

Sliding Hill — 11
Ghost Lights of Sliding Hill —**Mason County**

TNT Bunker Area — 15
Mothman —**Mason County**

Historic Lowe Hotel — 20
Historic Hotel Ghosts —**Mason County**

North Bend Rail Trail—Silver Run Tunnel — 21
The White Woman of Silver Run —**Ritchie County**

West Virginia Penitentiary in Moundsville — 25
Where All the Scary Ghosts End Up —**Marshall County**

Mount Welcome Cemetery — 30
Ikie's Tomb —**Pleasants County**

The Blennerhassett Hotel — 36
Elegant Ghost of Blennerhassett Hotel —**Wood County**

Blennerhassett Island Historical State Park — 38
Margaret Blennerhassett Walks the Shore —**Wood County**

Blennerhassett Island Historical State Park — 40
UGH! An Ohio River Monster —**Wood County**

Fort Boreman Scenic Overlook—Mountwood Park — 41
Spirits of Fort Boreman —**Wood County**

Boreman Wheel House — 42
Spirited Voice —**Wood County**

Quincy Park — 43
Ghostly Moans at Quincy Park —**Wood County**

Riverview Cemetery—Captain Deming Grave — 44
Return of the Captain —**Wood County**

Riverview Cemetery—Jackson Monument — 45
Weeping Woman of West Virginia —**Wood County**

Mustapha Island — 46
Burning Ghost —**Wood County**

Marrtown — 48
Banshee of Marrtown —**Wood County**

Old Click's Ford — 50
The Headless Soldier of Donohew Lane —**Jackson County**

West Virginia Ghost Stories, Legends, and Haunts 5

Table of Contents—West Virginia Ghost/Legends

Grasslick Creek — 52
The Pfost Family Massacre —Jackson County

Ravenswood Cemetery — 57
Devil Baby —Jackson County

Old Baltimore and Ohio Tracks — 58
Mysterious Echoes of Christmas Past —Jackson County

Ghost Pond/Haunted North Bend Rail Trail — 60
Ghost Pond on the Long Run —Doddridge County

Northeastern West Virginia

Trans-Allegheny Lunatic Asylum — 65
Trans-Allegheny Lunatic Asylum —Lewis County

Flinderation Tunnel — 67
Dead People Above, Dead People Below —Harrison County

Harpers Ferry/Shepherdstown

Harpers Ferry — 71
Map of Ghostly Places —Jefferson County

Harpers Ferry: Harper Museum (Harper House) — 72
The Face in the Window—Rachel Harper —Jefferson County

Harpers Ferry: Wager House — 75
The Ghosts of Wager House —Jefferson County

Harpers Ferry: Camp Hill — 77
Camp Hill Marching Ghost Troops —Jefferson County

Harpers Ferry: Harper Cemetery — 80
Strange Goings-On at a Cemetery —Jefferson County

Harpers Ferry: Old Railroad Tracks by U.S. Armory — 81
Screaming Jenny —Jefferson County

Harpers Ferry: John Brown's Fort — 83
John Brown's Raid on Harpers Ferry— —Jefferson County

Harpers Ferry: Hog Alley — 89
Dangerfield Newby's Heroic Sacrifice to Save his family—And His Sad Return —Jefferson County

Harpers Ferry: Maryland Heights — 92
Little Campfire Lights at Maryland Heights —Jefferson County

Harpers Ferry: Town House — 94
Ghost of the Drummer Boy —Jefferson County

Table of Contents—West Virginia Ghost/Legends

Harpers Ferry: Old Iron Horse Inn   95
Ghost of a Soldier Spy   —Jefferson County

Harpers Ferry: Brick Building   97
Crying Baby   —Jefferson County

Harpers Ferry: St. Peter's Roman Catholic Church   99
Father Michael Stays Behind   —Jefferson County

Harpers Ferry/Bolivar: Bolivar Heights Battlefield   102
Phantom Soldiers-Battle of Bolivar Heights—Jefferson County

Harpers Ferry: Hilltop House Hotel and Overlook   103
Banging Pots   —Jefferson County

Harpers Ferry: The Point at the Rivers   104
The Dead Peddler's Warning   —Jefferson County

John Brown Farmhouse Headquarters   106
Ghosts of the Lost Raid   —Washington County, MD

Antietam National Battlefield   107
Bloody Lane   —Washington County, MD

Burnside's Bridge   111
Eerie Blue Balls of Light   —Washington County, MD

Battle of Shepherdstown   112
Little Coin Left by a Ghost   —Jefferson County

The Entler Hotel—Historic Shepherdstown Museum   115
Ghost of Peyton Smith at Old Globe Tavern —Jefferson County

Jefferson Security Bank - Yellow Brick Road Restaurant   117
The Ghost at Table 25   —Jefferson County

Shepherdstown Sweet Shop & Bakery   118
Ghosts of an Old Battlefield Hospital   —Jefferson County

McMurran Hall   120
Old Man in the Clock Tower   —Jefferson County

The Entler-Weltzheimer House   121
The Dead Cobbler   —Jefferson County

New Street   123
The Ghost of Susie Ferrell   —Jefferson County

Table of Contents—West Virginia Ghost/Legends

Southeastern West Virginia

Big Bend Tunnel 126
Legend of John Henry —**Summers County**

Site of Morris Massacre 129
Morris Massacre —**Nicholas County**

Laurel Creek Ford by Panther Mountain 132
Ghost Dog of Laurel Creek Ford —**Nicholas County**

Peter's Creek Valley 136
Ghost left behind from the Skirmish in Summersville
—**Nicholas County**

Henry Young's Grave 139
Headless Ghost Rider of Powell Mountain —**Nicholas County**

Soule United Methodist Church and Cemetery 141
Greenbrier Ghost —Jailed By A Spirit —**Greenbrier County**

John Wesley United Methodist Church 147
A Church with Much Spirit —**Greenbrier County**

Historic General Lewis Inn 149
Lady in White —**Greenbrier County**

Greenbrier Resort 150
Ghosts Who Crave Luxury Even after Death
—**Greenbrier County**

Kate's Mountain Road 151
Kate's Mountain Bobbing Lights —**Greenbrier County**

Droop Mountain Battlefield 154
Dead Horses and Headless Soldiers on Droop Mountain
—**Pocahontas County**

Southwestern West Virginia

Camden Park 159
The Mound —**Cabell County**

The Office of Doctor Grimes 160
The Haunt of Lavina Wall —**Cabell County**

Fifth Street 161
Fifth Street Vanishing Hitchhiker —**Cabell County**

Frederick Hotel 163
Spirited Reflections of a Bootlegging Past —**Cabell County**

Table of Contents—West Virginia Ghost/Legends

Greater Huntington Cinema Theatre (Keith Albee)   164
The Lady in Red and the Shadow-Man   —Cabell County

Spring Hill Cemetery   165
Still Walking the Graves   —Cabell County

Woodmere Cemetery   166
Mother Blood   —Cabell County

Bridge and Short Streets   167
Woman in Black   —Cabell County

Guyandotte Cemetery   169
Wandering Ghost of Eleonore LeTulle   —Cabell County

Hawks Nest State Park   171
Legends of Lover's Leap   —Fayette County

Tracks Heading To the Ghost Town of Vanetta   175
Ghostly Lantern in Vanetta   —Fayette County

Railroad Tracks over Paint Creek   178
Fayette County Lights   —Fayette County

Glen Ferris Inn   179
An Inn's Ghostly Guest   —Fayette County

22 Mine Road   180
The Secret Life of Mamie Thurman   —Logan County

Hatfield-McCoy Country

Hatfield/McCoy Country   185
Spiritual Remains of Feuding Families—Hatfields and McCoys
   —Mingo County WV and Pike County Ky

Asa Harmon McCoy   187
Site of Asa Harmon McCoy's Killing   —Pike County, Ky

Hog Trial Cabin   188
The Pig Story   Pike County, Ky

Roseanna McCoy   189
The Lonely Grave of Roseanna's Baby   —Pike County, Ky

Paw Paw Tree Incident   192
Ghosts of the Paw Paw Tree Incident   —Pike County, Ky

The Old McCoy Homestead   193
The Fire   —Pike County, Ky

Battle of Grapevine Creek   195
The Last Battle and Hanging of Cotton Top   —Mingo County

Table of Contents—West Virginia Ghost/Legends

Dils Cemetery 198
The Graves of the McCoys —Pike County, Ky

Hatfield Cemetery 199
Devil Anse Rises —Logan County

Hatfield Tunnel 200
Hatfield Tunnel Creeping Crawler —Pike County, Ky

Grave of Octavia Hatcher 202
Octavia Hatcher—Buried Alive —Pike County, Ky

Ghosts of Matewan 205
Matewan Massacre —Mingo County

Ghosts of Matewan 210
Buskirk Cemetery—Smilin' Sid Hatfield —Pike County, Ky

Ghosts of Matewan 213
More Ghostly Places —Mingo County

Dingess Tunnel 214
Thrilling Ghostly Ride in Dingess Tunnel —Mingo County

Citations 216

Northwestern West Virginia

Sliding Hill
View at Scenic Overlook:
West Virginia Route 62
Letart, WV 25253
38.991252, -81.981632

Mason County

Ghost Lights of Sliding Hill

Sliding Hill, left, where ghostly lights are seen by travelers on WV-62 and boaters along the Ohio River, right. Syracuse is to the far right across the river. Hartford City is about a mile ahead.

If you live near Pomeroy, you have probably heard of the towns of Syracuse in Ohio, and Hartford City and New Haven in West Virginia. Hartford City and New Haven are nearly back to back, about a mile and a half apart. You could probably stand between the two towns along West Virginia Route 62 that runs through both and yell loud enough for somebody to hear you across the river in Syracuse.

There between the two West Virginia towns is a place called Sliding Bend Hill or, for short, Sliding Hill—a sheer-edged hill that dips downward and causes the river to come together at nearly right angles. This awkward angle made it a dangerous bend for steamboat pilots as the water hits the rocks with such speed, it was difficult to navigate.

Sliding Hill–from the Ohio side and along the Ohio River. A family living on the river and traveling downstream in their houseboat called a "shanty boat" or "junk boat" saw it years ago.

This dark recess had a ghost. Boatmen on the river and people traveling the roadway along the one and a half mile stretch of what is now West Virginia Route 62 reported seeing little lights dancing, ghosts, and even skeletons along Sliding Hill as far back as the late 1700s. In 1910, a family traveling south along the river in their houseboat anchored opposite Sliding Hill, unknowing of the mysterious lights. As dusk settled in the skies, the father began to see a strange light bobbing up and down the hillside. He grew suspicious of the light, silently slipped a skiff into the water, and paddled across. When he reached a position in the shadows, his eyes fell on a horrifying sight. He saw a huge headless monster shoving its weight into several large stones on the hillside just a short distance away. He made a hasty return, and in the dark of night, the family fled downriver in their shantyboat.

Reverend George Cleaton Wilding (1846 - 1925) was a Methodist circuit rider during the late 1800s and early 1900s who traveled the mountains of West Virginia preaching. When he was but a boy of ten around 1856, he lived in New Haven and worked as an errand boy for a store in Hartford. George often heard of the story of a haunting on Sliding Hill. But even at a tender age, he scoffed at the idea of ghosts. Back in those days, there was only a raggedy bridle path between New Haven and Hartford, and one day, still in the early hours of the morning, George was hurrying to work on this trail. Before him, he saw a colonial officer approaching him on horseback. The boy stopped and stared, mesmerized, and admiring the mighty horse and the grand uniform the rider wore, complete with a shiny sword at his belt. As the rider neared to less than 25 steps between the two and near a small creek of water trickling across the path, young George looked down long enough to jump across as not to get his shoes wet. When he looked up again, the rider had mysteriously vanished. So struck by the strange occurrence, the boy followed the trail to Hartford and found no hoofprints or sign that the rider had even passed!

The ghosts that step forth from twilight to the still hours of the night are those bearing lanterns to search fruitlessly for a hidden treasure. As the story goes, early settlers traveling along the Ohio River camped below the hill for the night. Within their boat, they carried many gold coins to buy some land. Unknown to them, thieves aware of their cargo had followed them. In the dark of night, while the party slept, the thieves came upon the boat and murdered the settlers. They secreted the bodies within a ledge and hid the gold coins until they could return for them at a safer, later date when suspicious fingers would not point at them for the raiding. They let the boat float on down the river.

Unfortunately for the murdering lot, they were all killed within the next year. However, on one thief's deathbed, he admitted to the murder and hiding the treasure. Not long after, the mysterious lights would begin. Later, many would search for the coins, but nobody found them. One by one, those who sought out the treasure were struck dead by some foul means and were cursed to come back in a ghostly form to search out the gold for eternity.

Sliding Hill—along WV-62 and facing toward New Haven.

TNT Bunker Area
*1335 Potters Creek Road
(2.2 miles from Route 62)
West Columbia, WV 25287
38.932298, -82.073468*

Watch for the guardrail and pull-off on the right. Walk just past the pond and to the first bunker hidden in the trees on the right.

Mason County

Mothman

Remote bunker area where Mothman was seen.

On Tuesday, November 15th, 1966, newlyweds Steve (age 20) and Mary Mallette (age 20) were joyriding about seven miles from their hometown of Point Pleasant with married couple Roger (age 18) and Linda Scarberry (age 19). The area they were driving in Scarberry's beloved black 1957 Chevy was the abandoned West Virginia Ordnance Works, locally nicknamed the TNT Area.

The power plant building where Mothman was seen. Image: Jeff Wamsley, author of Mothman: Behind the Red Eyes.

The Athens Messenger, November 18th, 1966—
Four young Point Pleasant residents return to the spot where an unusual creature was spotted earlier this week. The married couples Mr. and Mrs. Steve Mallette, left, and Mr. and Mrs. Roger Scarberry contend they found a "hoof-like" print in soft sand the next day. Staff photo by George Lovell. Photo courtesy The Athens Messenger.

Shortly before midnight, they spotted something large, about six to seven feet high, wobble-walking around an old power plant building. It was huge, grey, shaped like a muscular human, and had wings protruding from its back. Unfortunately, none of the witnesses got a clear look at the creature's face—the huge, red "glowing" eyes dominated the entire front of the head. In a panic, the terrified couples sped from the area. As one of the passengers called out that the creature was following them, Scarberry raced along the curvy road to town at up to 100 miles per hour on the straightaways. However, the winged beast kept pace and struck the side of the car. The couples later reported their wild tale to newspapers who dubbed the creature "Mothman."

Where the Mothman was seen. The creature was best described by Roger and Linda Scarberry and Steve and Mary Mallette who were at the TNT bunker area when they saw it. They described the creature as "a large flying man with ten-foot wings."

The incident began a wave of sightings. Most found it centered around the TNT area outside Point Pleasant. However, it was seen on both sides of the Ohio River and spotted outside Gallipolis, Ohio. In November 1966—Bob Bosworth and Alan Coates were riding motorcycles down Camp Conley Road (TNT Area) and decided to work their way over to the power plant. The two saw something on the roof of the old power plant building and stopped to check it out. They observed a huge 7-foot bird-like man fly off.

Thirteen-year-old Faye Dewitt-Leport and her siblings set off in a Ford truck to see the Mothman. During the drive, the creature appeared beside the vehicle, staring with wide, red eyes at the girl through the window. Her frightened brother sped down the road at nearly 50 miles per hour.

After sliding to a sideways stop on one sharp turn, the monster leaped on the hood of the truck and stared at them through the windshield. Then it bounded upward to the top of an abandoned building. Her brother immediately sprung from the truck and began tossing rocks and coal at the winged Mothman. The creature instantly shot down toward the boy, and he dove back into the vehicle, speeding away.

One of the lead reporters, Mary Hyre, from The Athens Messenger wrote this:

> **POINT PLEASANT** — Six—or maybe seven more people became believers in the Mason County Monster Wednesday night. What is it they saw? They don't know, but they have managed to convince a raft of people they saw something. The latest observers of the red-eyed, wing-backed six-foot thing are Mr. and Mrs. Raymond Wamsley; Ricky. Connie and Vickie Thomas and Marcella Bennett. They spotted the monster around 9 p. m. Wednesday outside the home of Mr. and Mrs. Ralph Thomas, in the TNT area, where the thing was sighted Tuesday night. Observer number seven is reported to be a Cheshire area youth who allegedly was chased by a thing matching the description of the Mason County Monster, The chase took place on Route 7 in Ohio. **Athens Messenger. NOV 17, 1966**

There are those who believe the creature dates back to a curse bestowed upon the area from the Shawnee Chief, Cornstalk. Cornstalk suffered a horrible defeat at the Battle of Point Pleasant when the Virginia militia and Indians from the Shawnee and Mingo tribes fought in 1774 along the Ohio River. Cornstalk was so distraught over the loss that he laid a curse on the land and the people who lived on it near Point Pleasant and Gallipolis. Some believe the Mothman incident ensured the completion of this curse.

Devout ufologists claim Mothman was an alien. Witnesses from 1966 reported strange UFOs in the sky above the TNT area and Point Pleasant during the time.

Some who sighted the Mothman believe the creature was placed there as a distraction for UFO activity taking place around the military base at the time. There were reports of the elusive Men in Black, black-suited government agents who mysteriously appeared and tried to silence witnesses and researchers during the strange event. Most who had an experience with the Mothman would also report an encounter with the men in black suits that later would frighten them more than the Mothman.

Monstrous winged creatures have preceded catastrophic events. The San Francisco earthquake, Hurricane Katrina, and even the 9/11 terrorist attacks on the United States all had similar reports of a strange flying creature appearing before the tragedy occurred. But nobody in Point Pleasant expected the sightings would lead up to the collapse of the Silver Bridge between Point Pleasant and Gallipolis on December 15th, 1967. Constructed in 1928 to span the Ohio River and connect the two towns, the bridge was crowded with holiday shoppers. One of the last truck drivers to cross the bridge before it fell into the frigid Ohio River reported spotting a massive winged creature circling the bridge. Forty-six people lost their lives that night. It was one of the worst disasters striking the area. The army later pulled 34 cars from the icy waters.

After the tragic event, most Mothman reports stopped, which led many to believe the disaster was the reason the creature appeared. However, the sightings have not ended completely. Once in a while, reports still surface of a Mothman-like creature near the bridge site or swooping above the TNT area outside Point Pleasant.

You can see him, too. Well, you can see a replica of him and other one-of-a-kind exhibits of Mothman by visiting the Mothman Museum in Point Pleasant, West Virginia—

400 Main St, Point Pleasant, WV 25550

Historic Lowe Hotel
401 Main Street
Point Pleasant WV 25550
38.842959, -82.138908

Mason County

Historic Hotel Ghosts

When the hotel opened in 1901 to accommodate travelers along the Ohio River, guests lodged on the upper floors. The lower floors housed businesses—a barbershop, bank, billiards room, and even a dance floor. Several ghosts have found a home at the hotel, including a young woman who dances in the mezzanine between floors. On the second floor, the full-bodied apparition of a child riding a tricycle makes a ghostly visit with wheels squealing a creepy *squeak-squeak-squeak* in the empty hallway. On the third floor, visitors have heard a soft whistling, and doors open and close. A long-dead riverboat captain, believed to be James O'Brien of the Homer Smith, a regular excursion steamboat popular along this route of the Ohio River, has been seen in room 316 looking out the window toward the river.

Silver Run Tunnel
Silver Run Road
(Co Rd 31/4)
North Bend Rail Trail
Cairo, WV 26337
39.207692, -81.196644

Ritchie County

The White Woman of Silver Run

Silver Run Tunnel

There is a legend about a young woman who haunts the old Baltimore and Ohio tracks just outside Cairo. In 1910, a young engineer made the 169-mile midnight westbound express run along the Baltimore and Ohio tracks starting in Grafton heading toward Clarksburg and then Parkersburg. It was a long run, and it was dark along much of the route. The track between the few tiny towns was surrounded on both sides by blasted out rock, forest, and steep hillsides.

Bring a flashlight. It is a long, dark hike through the tunnel.

All was well the first 24 or so miles from Grafton to Clarksburg. It was not until about 58 miles later things began to change in a very horrifying way. When the engineer came upon the short stretch of the railway at the entrance to Tunnel #19, in the light of the moon and headlights, he saw a woman in a pale dress with raven-colored hair walking along the tracks. Horrified he would hit her, he tried desperately to stop the train by throwing the brakes into emergency. He could not stop in time. The engineer would later report to watchmen at the Smithburg Tunnel about 36 miles west that he and the fireman jumped from the train, but a layer of fog on the tracks seemed to swallow up the pale lady.

If that were not enough, the engineer would see her again on his westbound express. It would be the next half-moon before she appeared. This time he caught the details of her clothing—golden slippers, black hair, and a jeweled brooch. When the train drew its warning whistle, a moan came from the deepest depths of the mysterious woman.

Rumors of the ghostly woman spread. Other engineers along the track began to see her. Trains slowed near the Silver Run Tunnel #19 to avoid her, many nearly wrecking to keep from hitting her. A stalwart Irishman by the name of O'Flannery scoffed at the ghost stories. But it would not be long before she came to him along the tracks on a cool autumn night, disappearing into the heavy fog. After he stopped the train and searched around, O'Flannery vowed that if he saw her while driving the train again, there was no way he would slow his run down. He would simply not stop. Instead, O'Flannery would barrel right through her.

And one night, Engineer O'Flannery did. Along his run, the ghostly phantom of Silver Run Tunnel #19 showed herself at the tunnel entrance. Just as he promised, O'Flannery drove the train right through the woman. He watched in awe as she screamed and flew into the air. However, when he pulled into Parkersburg, he would get a terrible fright. Bystanders along the track, signalmen, agents, and section men were desperately waving him down. It appears along the long route between the tunnel and Parkersburg that railway workers sent telegraph reports advising other stations that a girl was riding perched on the cowcatcher on the front of the train.

When the railroad agents inquired about the pale woman in white showing up along the tunnel, they found a young woman who had disappeared 25 years earlier on her way to Parkersburg. She never arrived. Many years after the engineers reported seeing the ghost, someone found a skeleton buried in the cellar of an old house near the Silver Run Tunnel #19. Along with the bones were a brooch and golden slippers. Over the years that followed, more rail men saw the White Woman of Silver Run. They swore they could hear her moan near the tunnel while the train whistled its warning.

You can try to see and hear her too. The old train track is part of West Virginia's North Bend Rail Trail.

Directions: Go into Cairo (39.208700, -81.157362) and then place this GPS code: (39.20768, -81.19665) into GPS. Honestly, if you do not, you will be on old roads best suited for ATVs. But the road in Cairo will lead out of town along two steel bridges and then a narrow gravel road called Silver Run Road. The pull-off is right here on the left of the trail and has room for one car. Walk south (away from Cairo) along North Bend Rail Trail, about 10 minutes hike on gravel.

Or you can park at the pull-off in Cairo and walk the 2-3 miles to the tunnel. Tunnel is along the North Bend Rail Trail.

The pull-off before the tunnel.

West Virginia Penitentiary in Moundsville
818 Jefferson Avenue
Moundsville, WV 26041
39.916785, -80.742687

Marshall County

Where All the Scary Ghosts End Up

West Virginia State Penitentiary in Moundsville.

The West Virginia State Penitentiary in Moundsville had its beginnings in 1863 when West Virginia seceded Virginia to join the Union. A prison was needed for the new state to house those who broke the law. It operated from 1876 to 1995. Inmate labor was used in building the mammoth, formidable fortress made of stones quarried from Marshall and Wetzel counties and stretching three blocks long.

Authorities set up the entire prison operation as self-sufficient. There was a wagon and carpentry shop, stone yard, brickyard, blacksmith, tailor, bakery, hospital, and even a coal mine nearby. When a prisoner arrived at the penitentiary, they were provided with a serial number, bathed, given a haircut and shave, and supplied with a gray prison uniform. After a medical examination, wardens photographed inmates and recorded their complete personal history. Able-bodied inmates were required to work 9 hours a day except for Saturday afternoon, Sundays, and holidays.

During a tour, we could explore inside the jail cells, and they closed the doors so we could feel what it was like to be locked inside. The cells were so small—5 feet by 7 feet, we could stand in the center, hold out our arms, and just about touch both walls. Note the two cots along the wall. When the prison was at its peak with prisoners, there were at least three in each cell. Thirty seconds with the door closed and I wanted out!

It was the worst offenders walking through the doors of the prison—thieves, murderers, and dangerous criminals. People died here. From 1899 to 1959, there were 94 men executed at the prison, 85 of these would be hanged.

Hangings were considered an event with a festival-like atmosphere, and the public was invited to attend. That is until police arrested 54-year-old Frank Hyer, who had barricaded himself in his restaurant after beating his wife, Eva, to death. After a battle of tear-gas, an arrest, and prosecution, authorities hanged him in prison on December 19th, 1930. However, his body weight was so great that the rope decapitated him as he fell through the trap door of the gallows. After that, attendance was by invitation only.

The first building constructed was the North Wagon Gate, above.

To left: It is also where men were hanged. Note the scaffold on the ceiling, center.

In 1973, five guards were held hostage during a riot. One inmate was stabbed to death. On New Year's Day in 1986, a second riot lasted two days. Three inmates died. Weird things tend to happen here. A man named Avril Paul Adkins had to be hanged twice. The first time, he fell and landed on his head. There were at least 36 murders inside the walls. Robert Daniel Wall—inmate 44670 (also known as R.D.) was a maintenance worker who cared for the boiler room. He was in the jail for a Logan County rape conviction but was a favorite of the warden and kept an eye out on the prisoners.

He was also a snitch. R.D. Wall was murdered on October 8th, 1979, in the boiler room, and his face now appears on the walls and as a green mist in photos.

Left: The boiler room where Wall was murdered, hacked to death by prisoners.

The shower house and cells. When I took a closer look, there is a shadow figure watching me complete with 1800s jacket and pants. Oh, my.

The Moundsville Prison offers tours, and it is definitely worth the trip. The building has lots of history and ghost stories, and every bit is made interesting enough to keep a 9-year-old's attention. Chuck Ghent, a former correctional officer from 1986 to 1995, offers stories of the prison's past that leave the visitors hanging with bated breath.

Now, West Virginia State Penitentiary in Moundsville offers day-guided historical and paranormal tours and special events. One event, a haunted attraction around Halloween, is so terrifying that kids under 13-years-old are discouraged from attending the event because it is not just the costumed characters joining in the Halloween fun.

A couple of years ago, at the last minute, one of the tour guides at the yearly Halloween event decided to join a group ready to be guided through the maze of fear after her shift. Because it is pitch black, to move from one area to the next, guests latch on to the person in front of them as a guide. Like a long caterpillar, they are led into the dark, hoping they do not lose the connection with the person in front of them. When the lights turned out this time, the group milling around latched on to one another. The off-duty tour guide turned to join the group, her hand clasping the shoulder in front of her. She felt a hand fasten to her shoulder, cold fingers tickling her neck.

The group wound their way through the torturous darkness clinging to each other for safety, finally ending into the light. The off-duty tour guide had laughed softly to herself. She was familiar with all of those working as costumed characters, so she was not scared at their pranks. She had chuckled a bit under her breath at the screams of the guests in front of her. As she felt the release of the hand to her shoulder, she turned automatically to address the person who had held her shoulder the entire time. And she jolted. No one was behind her! Who or *what* had been walking with a hand on her shoulder for the last twenty minutes? Perhaps somebody (or something) who was getting the last laugh!

Mount Welcome Cemetery
*Off Mount Welcome Road
Arvilla, WV 26146*
This is private property and
you must ask permission to visit!

Pleasants County

Ikie's Tomb

When Isaac "Ikie" Mooring, who lived near Algeria, died at age 7 years and two months, his distraught parents—40-year-old Kenneth (an oil/gas driller) and 29-year-old Emma Jane had him interred in a coffin. The couple placed the coffin in a specially-built family mausoleum, complete with glass windows and doors, at Mount Welcome Cemetery.

West Virginia Ghost Stories, Legends, and Haunts 31

It was not just any coffin. Ikie's parents purchased one of the much-advertised and quite expensive glass caskets that, one newspaper stated, was filled with a solution of alcohol after placing his body inside to preserve it. It was fitting. Ikie's death was unexpected.

Corpse In a Glass Casket.
Kenneth Moering of Algeria, whose seven-year-old son Isaac died in Parkersburg, W. Va., a short time ago from eating poisoned ice cream, has had the boy's body placed in a glass casket, which is filled with alcohol, says a Parkersburg dispatch to the New York World. The latter has preserved the body, while the glass casket enables the parents to see the features of their son at any time. The casket is in a mausoleum, and the parents say the body will always be kept as it is now, so that they can always behold the face of their son.

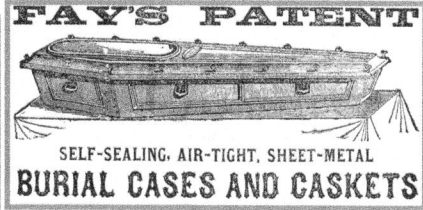

Advertisement for Fay's Patent from Williams Cincinnati City Directory, one of many specialty coffins designed to preserve.

The Massillon Evening Independent, Wednesday August 17th, 1904 noting Ikie's glass casket. Perhaps an incited sales pitch by the glass casket company who designed his little casket.

Above: Here is a glass casket if you've never seen one. This tiny casket was dug up in a basement while renovating a home in San Francisco (The home was built over previously vacated land of the Odd Fellows Cemetery).

Left: Edith Cook —Garden of Innocence provides burials for abandoned and unidentified children. They were able to find the identity of the child in the above casket, 2-year-old Edith Cook, who died in 1876! She was almost perfectly preserved as would Ikie had his tomb not been vandalized. Images courtesy: Garden of Innocence.

He had died of milk poisoning from eating ice cream—milk poisoning or milk sickness occurs when milking cows graze on White Snakeroot (usually when foraging woodlands because hay is unavailable) and a person drinks the milk or a milk product. Its after-effects are like a horrible gut-puking stomach virus and can be deadly. In Ikie's case, the sweet treat proved fatal.

His grandpa wrote this obituary for him in the March 18th, 1904, Pleasants County Leader:

"'Ikie' Mooring, the beautiful little boy and the only child of Kenneth and Emma J. Mooring, died March 3rd, 1904, aged seven years and two months. 'Ikie' is not dead, only a most beautiful, sweet flower that shed forth its sweet fragrance here for so short a time, has been plucked and transported in the fields of paradise, there to bloom forever. In his short life here, he touched and sweetened the lived of all who knew him, bound himself around the hearts of dear ones with cords of love that can never be severed. Now he stands on the other shore and holds in his angelic hands the Life Line, and beckons loved ones to come to him. He says to his dear Papa and Mama, 'I cannot come to you, but you can come to me; hold on to the Life Line, and we shall be housed together again in this beautiful land where there is no death, no sorrow, nor broken hearts, but one eternal life of joy, peace, and love."

After the family laid Ikie to rest, his mourning mother would often visit the grave, bringing with her some of her son's cherished items like a bicycle and schoolbooks that she left within the tomb, closing the door gently behind her when she left. Like many grief-stricken parents, Emma Jane would talk to her dead son, filling him in on the day's activities as she swept and cleaned the brush away from the interior and exterior of the mausoleum.

Ikie's Tomb, now nearly hidden in the overgrown forest barring the occasional pack of trespassing ATV riders digging a path straight through the cemetery, and in my case, nearly running me over as I quietly viewed the graves.

Ikie's mother had three other children at the time who had not made it through childhood. Older locals who remember the stories of Ikie said that their bodies, too, were interred within the tomb in stone crocks. Some had even heard local lore saying that Emma Jane sorrowed over her little boy so intensely, she would pull off the lid to the casket, wheedle the boy's body from within, and rock him in a chair she had brought to the tomb, crooning to him as if he was asleep.

His burial clothes were a little striped sailor suit. When she would leave to go home, those seeing her along the road would note blue and white stains dribbling down her dress! Oh, and there were always rumors that when she cleaned, she would take the little children from their caskets and hang them by their collars to tree limbs to let them dry!

Ikie's newer grave, center, tucked gently between his loving family. To visit the grave, you will need to ask the landowner's permission.

Time would pass, and the family moved out of the quiet community. Ikie remained, but as the years went by, the mausoleum fell into disrepair. And Ikie's little coffin began to fall apart. For their time, glass caskets filled with alcohol or other preserving liquid were top of the line. However, the very fluid used to preserve the body—alcohol—was the demise of the casket, eventually causing the rubber seal on the window to deteriorate, and such, the alcohol would evaporate exposing the body to the elements and decay. Eventually, vandals and animals worked their way into the tomb. Dogs dragged Ikie's body out into the woods, and hunters finally found it, who contacted authorities. Now, Ikie's final resting place is outside the mausoleum near grandparents—Mary Ann and Oliver Gorrell and Uncle Ralph, who died of pneumonia.

So now, barring the ATVs careening through the cemetery, Ikie rests in peace. His tomb is closed except the windows (and the roof), so no more vandals can desecrate his old grave. Not so for his devoted mama who, like any good mama, has a love for her child lasting an eternity. Folks have seen her hovering around the tomb, still keeping her son company even after death. Some say they hear soft crooning inside the mausoleum, but when they peer inside the window, no one is there. Rest in peace, you two, rest in peace.

Peering through the window to the crypt. For years, Ikie's toys and bike were inside. Now, they are gone.

The Blennerhassett Hotel
320 Market Street
Parkersburg, WV 26101
39.264984, -81.561633

Elegant Ghost of Blennerhassett Hotel

The Blennerhassett Hotel. *Courtesy Library of Congress*

The Blennerhassett Hotel offers comfy accommodations along with a few friendly spirits. Ghosts at the hotel include a well-dressed gentleman in an old-fashioned, three-piece grey suit, a top hat, and cane. Guests and staff who have witnessed him state he has slicked-back hair and a beard.

Investigators believe he is the friendly ghost of William Chancellor, the man who built the hotel in 1889. He likes to watch over the building.

Listen for the quiet patter of ghostly children's feet in the hallways.

The second floor hosts playful ghostly children who might pop up to tease you and vanish as quickly as they came. The Blennerhassett website notes a bellman who admitted seeing a little girl in a fancy dress out of the corner of his eye. And another heard a ghostly whistle. On the lower level near the elevator, a little boy dressed in turn of the century clothing tugs gently on shirts. Then, there is the 4 o'clock Knocker, another playful spirit who knocks on the doors in the early morning.

A man in a white tuxedo sometimes makes an appearance in hotel mirrors. Staff have heard laughter and chatter coming from the Charleston Ballroom.

Regardless if you come for a stay to simply relax in luxury, or you are looking for ghosts, you will be happy you visited the Blennerhassett. The accommodations are quite comfortable, and the food, great. We even got a gentle knock on our door the night we stayed there. I thought it was one of my kids giggling inside our room right after. However, both were sound asleep in their beds, and no one was in the hallway!

Blennerhassett Island Historical State Park
Boat: 137 Juliana Street
Parkersburg, WV 26101
39.264914, -81.565030

Wood County

Margaret Blennerhassett Walks the Shore

Blennerhassett Mansion.

Attorney Harman Blennerhassett and his wife Margaret purchased an island just outside Parkersburg in the middle of the Ohio River and built a mansion with lavish gardens in 1798. In 1806, the couple was involved in Aaron Burr's treasonous conspiracy against the United States. Burr convinced Harman to be a part of a rebellion to start an independent country in the western part of the U.S.

Harman spent most of a fortune willed to him when his father died building boats to transport Burr's followers to his new empire. However, Harman was caught and jailed. He was later released, but the failed attempt of rebellion left the family in financial ruin. The couple would live in poverty for the rest of their lives.

The mansion burned in 1811, but in the 1980s, the state rebuilt it as a tourist attraction on the island. Although Margaret Blennerhassett died in a poorhouse in New York, she returns to her beloved home nowadays as a ghostly figure who walks the shoreline. The smell of lavender and even the scent of the horses she loved to ride slips into the air not far behind the ghost. Some have seen her with a young daughter who died on the island and whose gravesite location is unidentified.

Take a boat ride across the Ohio River to the island and watch for Margaret Blennerhassett's ghost strolling the island shoreline. Or take a carriage ride tour and look for spirited remains of the island's past.

The state park offers boat rides to the island for a small fee seasonally, carriage rides, and tours of the home. Do not forget to visit the Blennerhassett Museum in Parkersburg (where you purchase boat tickets). It has many interesting and creepy artifacts!

Blennerhassett Island
Historical State Park
Boat: 137 Juliana Street
Parkersburg, WV 26101
39.264914, -81.565030

Wood County

UGH! An Ohio River Monster

Ugh! An Ohio River Monster! That is what the Special Dispatch to the Cincinnati Enquirer announced on July 2nd, 1893 about these waters near Blennerhassett Island.

In 1893, boaters in the Ohio River between Neal Island and Blennerhassett Island were stunned to discover a horrifying sea serpent moving around in the water and rounding their small skiff. It was ten feet long, black, and with eyes larger than a big dog. Thinking it was a hoax, another party of boaters went out into the water and were shocked to see the same creature floating nearby. For a short time, there was such a scare that the newspapers proclaimed social boating clubs would be at a huge discount until someone killed the sea serpent!

Fort Boreman Scenic Overlook
Fort Boreman Drive
Parkersburg, WV 26101
39.260714, -81.568843

Wood County

Spirits of Fort Boreman

Fort Boreman was built in 1863 because of its vantage point and to protect the railroad facilities during the Civil War. Union soldiers garrisoned here until 1865. Land nearby held a pest house/cemetery for epidemics. Before the park road entrance, a scaffold was set up and used to hang Thomas Boise, Mortimer Gibbony, and Daniel Grogan, who murdered Abram Deem, a local farmer/southern sympathizer. Hikers have long seen misty figures walking the grounds and spectral voices talking from the hilltop, ghostly signs of the land's many uses in the past.

Boreman Wheel House
406 Avery Street
Parkersburg, WV 26101
39.264247, -81.560239

Spirited Voice

Boreman Wheel House.

West Virginia's first governor, Arthur Boreman, built this house around 1863 to live by his daughter—his home was across the street. Witnesses hear voices and footsteps and have seen a ghostly light-haired man in one room. During the Civil War, the military used a building next to the Boreman House as a hospital. Some speculate that the strange sounds and sights are leftover from soldiers who died there and wandered to the Boreman House.

Quincy Park
1000 Quincy Street
Parkersburg, WV 26101
39.267456, -81.552663

Wood County

Ghostly Moans at Quincy Park

Quincy Park, overlooking the town.

Doctors used Quincy Park as an overflow tent hospital for 500 to 1000 African American and Irish American soldiers during the Civil War. Theresa Racer, who writes Theresa's Haunted History of the Tri-State, reports that many here died when a smallpox epidemic hit the camp. The moans of the sick were heard all the way downtown. Now, their ghostly cries ride the wind, and on some days, you can hear them in the park and along the hillside.

Riverview Cemetery
Captain Deming Grave
1341 Juliana Street
Parkersburg, WV 26101
39.273215, -81.553639

Wood County

Return of the Captain

Fifty-four-year-old Captain George Deming, a master mariner, was buried in Riverview Cemetery on April 21st, 1861. Originally from Hartford, Connecticut, he moved to Parkersburg at the time of the Civil War. His tombstone is engraved with a ship and next to it are smaller graves believed to be his children. One is Nena, who was born less than a year after he died, and another is marked simply: *G.D.* The long-dead captain visits the graves, seen in dark clothing and hovering near a chain-link fence nearby.

Riverview Cemetery Jackson Monument
1341 Juliana Street
Parkersburg, WV 26101
39.273215, -81.553639

Wood County

Weeping Woman of West Virginia

There are many legends surrounding the statue that guards the Jackson Family graves. Some claim to have seen the weeping woman statue move. Others report that it will grant a wish to those pure of heart. Women trying to conceive who have touched her hand gently claim to have become pregnant within the year!

Mustapha Island
Harris, WV 26181
View: 39.214240, -81.728987
Island: 39.209277, -81.728848

Wood County

Burning Ghost

Wreck of the Steamboat Kanawha. Courtesy Cincinnati Library.

On the blustery Wednesday evening of January 5th, 1916, the steam packet Kanawha was carrying freight and passengers from Pittsburgh to Charleston along the flooded Ohio River. After leaving Little Hocking, it set its course onward. As the boat came to Lock 19, the river was so high that the lock was submerged, and the high winds made it difficult to steer. The hull rammed into a barely submerged steel light tower at the lock, leaving a gaping hole in the boat. The steamer turned over; up to 16 people drowned.

Mustapha Island, on a cold January day where lights are seen.

In 1917, a steamboat captain on the R. Dunbar began seeing lights hovering around Mustapha Island, a small Ohio River island downstream from the lock where the tragic accident occurred. They appeared like lanterns signaling with a wave and bobbing around in unseen hands, and most believed they were the ghosts of those who drowned in the steam packet Kanawha accident. Other steamboat captains following the river started seeing the yellowish glow of lantern lights there too. Boaters noted the lights bouncing around the island well into the 1930s. The Pittsburgh Press—August 8th, 1939 comments that passengers on the Gordon C. Greene steamer were still seeing the lights each night while they passed by the island.

The Burning Ghost. There's a fine ghost on the Gordon Greene whenever she plies between Cincinnati and Pittsburgh—the ghost of Mustapha Island. Years ago a boat sunk at this spot and many persons were drowned. Some weeks after, a pilot was passing when he saw someone on shore waving a lantern. Believing it a signal, he steered the boat to land, but when he reached the shore, the light had vanished. Thinking he was mistaken, he moved out to the river again. And instantly the light reappeared. The mysterious light showed regularly after that and is still visible on every clear night to the Gordon Greene passengers. Sometimes it is like a flashlight, sometimes it is like a torch, sometimes it is like a man carrying a lantern. . .
The Pittsburgh Press August 8th, 1939.

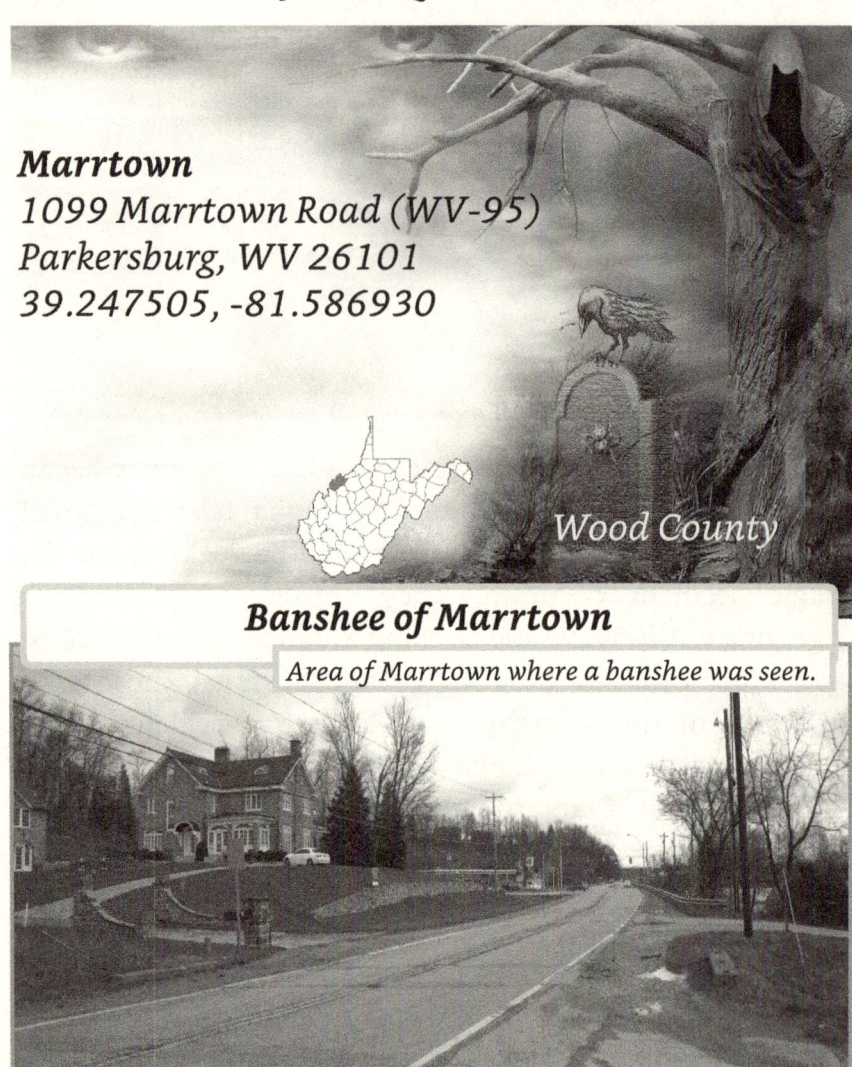

Marrtown
1099 Marrtown Road (WV-95)
Parkersburg, WV 26101
39.247505, -81.586930

Wood County

Banshee of Marrtown

Area of Marrtown where a banshee was seen.

A banshee is a fairy or female spirit who wails or keens, heralding the death of a person. The Irish called them Bean Sidhe-she dressed in a gray cape, green dress, and had weepy eyes from crying. The Scottish called these fairy folk Bean Nigh– she is usually seen as an old woman in raggedy clothing squatting in desolate creeks washing the bloody clothing and grave shrouds of those who will soon die.

When the Irish and the Scottish settled in Ohio and West Virginia, they did not come alone. They also brought with them the spirits and lore of their ancestors to establish roots in the areas they lived. Such, entered the *banshee* into an area just outside Parkersburg.

Just a little less than two miles from Parkersburg, sits Marrtown. The founder of this little town, Thomas Marr, was haunted by a banshee. Many think this entity a ghost. However, the banshee is a female spirit or fairy that warns of impending death. Several times while riding to work at the Baltimore and Ohio Railroad freight yard in 1874, 61-year-old Marr was followed by a rider in a raggedy hood that would vanish from sight. He told his wife, Mary, this strange story, and little was thought of it until the evening a rider came to the back gate of the home. When Mary went out to welcome the guest, the rider dressed in dark, ragtag clothing and hood disappeared into the night. It was February 6th, 1874. Thomas Marr was found dead at the freight depot hours later. He had climbed to the top of the station box to clean out a stovepipe, fell, and broke his neck.

> **Killed. Thomas Marr**, for the last sixteen years the watchful and efficient guardian of the property of the B. & O.R.R.Co at the lower depot, was found lying opposite his station box, a little before five o'clock yesterday morning with his neck broken and dead. It seems that he took a step ladder from the freight office at half past four, and, as is supposed, went upon the roof to clean out his stove pipe. He must have missed his footing and fell to the ground, a distance of perhaps ten feet. He was a genial old man of near sixty years, and seemed particularly cheerful... **Parkersburg Examiner, February 7th, 1874**

Stories are told the banshee returned to wail when Mary died at age ninety. Some believe the creature still remains in this area. There have been reports of a woman wearing a ragged, black cape walking along WV-95 at Parkersburg near the W.H. Bickel Estate during bad weather. Whether she forewarns people of impending death or is just a ghostly reminder of the past is unknown. But it is fair warning that during thunderstorms or when feeling a bit ill, avoid that area at all costs!

Old Click's Ford
WV-331
Cottageville, WV 25239
38.863870, -81.853429

Jackson County

The Headless Soldier of Donohew Lane

The area of George Click's ford where local militia force-marched Stewart Donohew (also spelled Donohue) to his death.

In November of 1862, Union soldier Private Stewart Donohew took a leave to his home on Little Mill Creek from his volunteer position with Company K, 9th Regiment of the West Virginia Infantry. The 55-year-old man had enrolled in March of 1862. He returned home for medical reasons, but paperwork was filed stating he had not been present at roll call in September and October and such had deserted.

On November 10th, 1862, neighbors warned him that a group of local home guards had been sent to arrest him as a deserter. The news left him ill at ease, but Donohew set out to meet the home guards to deny the accusations and such, ran into the small group of men not far from his home. As not to alarm the home guards, he slipped his gun into an old stump and allowed them to escort him to Cottageville unarmed so he could explain his leave of absence in a hearing. A mile east of Mt Alto in an area called Dutch Ridge, the group slowed to cross Little Mill Creek. It was just as they traversed Click's Ford, a crossing on the old George Click property over Little Mill Creek, one of the guards, a local man by the name of Job Snyders, shot Donohew in the back. Donohew died two days later.

It was not long after that individuals traversing Little Mill Creek began to see strange and unexplainable things where the home guard murdered Donohew. He appeared as a young horse to some and others, a brownish ball of powder. A minister traveling through the area reported seeing a headless soldier clambering over a wooden fence. The brother of Stewart Donahew stated he met Stewart on the lane after dusk. It scared him so badly he ran to the flood-swollen creek and jumped in, swimming across.

Authorities never punished the murderer. It is the reason Stewart Donohew walks the area of Old Click's Ford, now next to a thick concrete bridge crossing the creek. You might see him there if you drive across along WV-331. Just as passersby saw him in the 1860s, he comes in different forms—an animal, a brownish ball of powder, or a full-body apparition begging to explain his absence and get restitution from the man who murdered him on a lonely stretch of road over Little Mill Creek.

Grasslick Creek
Grasslick Road
Ripley, WV 25271
38.71281, -81.64232

The Pfost Family Massacre

Near the area where an old homestead once stood along Grasslick Creek and ghostly cries for help are heard.

In November of 1897, 61-year-old Chloe Pfost-Greene lived with her three children from different marriages – Jimmy Greene—age 18; Matilda Pfost—age 26; and Alice Pfost—age 28 in a homestead along Grasslick Creek in Jackson County, West Virginia. She was well known in the community, always giving a helping hand to those in need and offering a bed to anyone needing a place to stay.

The Pfost property from the pamphlet: Slaughter of the Pfost-Greene Family by O.J. Morrison

Chloe Pfost-Greene.

One such young man she nurtured was John Morgan, who was left an orphan at the early age of nine or ten. For five years, he lived with the family until he married in 1896. However, Morgan would stop in occasionally to earn money helping around the farm. Chloe Pfost-Greene would not let Morgan or his new wife go hungry—she always sent the man home with bread or grain to help support them. She had developed such a caring attitude to her foster son that she had given John Morgan a horse. He had traded it in the spring for two younger horses and a loan note of $35.00, which was coming due.

A strange incident transpired on Friday, October 29th. John Morgan awakened the family at one in the morning, insisting that Jimmy, Chloe's son, go raccoon hunting with him. A few yards from their home, Morgan asked Jimmy if they had yet to sell a horse they had advertised for sale.

Jimmy told him no, they had not, but they were sure to do so by the next day. Then oddly, Morgan called off the raccoon hunt. Although Jimmy mentioned the odd behavior to his family and suggested Morgan might steal the money, it seemed to raise no great alarm.

On the cool Tuesday night of November 2nd at around 6:00 p.m., Morgan stopped again at the Pfost-Greene home. This time, it was with the request to have Chloe cut his hair. Unable to do it that evening, she allowed him to spend the night so she could take care of him in the morning.

That night, John Morgan bunked with Jimmy. Around four in the morning on November 3rd, 1897, both arose, and Morgan followed the young man out to the hog pen on his customary chore of feeding the farm animals. Morgan waited for the young man to turn, picked up a hatchet and stone at the small pigsty, and beat Jimmy to death. He then returned to the house to find the two sisters cooking breakfast while their mother tidied up her bedroom. Immediately, he struck Alice with the hatchet and then turned to Matilda and hit her twice with the same weapon.

Believing both women were dead, Morgan proceeded to the bedroom and burst through the door, where he eventually murdered Chloe after a brutal battle that ended at the front door. Alice and Matilda were not dead—Matilda crawled to the sitting room where they found her corpse later. Alice escaped by hiding in a woodpile at the hen house while her sister begged her to grab the gun. Alice could do no more than flee for help to the nearby neighbor's home.

Authorities apprehended John Morgan, and a jury found him guilty. He hanged in December for his crime. They found no true motive for the murders, barring he needed money to repay the loan for the horse. Morgan's wife had complained to neighbors that for about six months, he had appeared depressed and talked and hummed to himself.

Hanging of John Morgan.

Newspaper article of the slaughter.

TRIPLE MURDER—Most Cold Blooded Crime in the Annals of the State. **FOR PURPOSES OF ROBBERY**—An Aged Woman, Her Son, and Daughter, Living Near Ripley, Jackson County Fall Victims to the Murderer's Lust for Gold-Another Daughter Seriously Injured by the Fiend-He is Captured In the Woods Near the Scene of the Crime and Lodged in Jail-The Victims Prominently Connected— Parkersburg, W. Va. Nov 3 Details of one of the most horrible crimes in the annals of the state were received here this evening from Jackson county, and from reports a "lynching bee" is very probably before morning. Eight miles southeast of Ripley, in the isolated locality of Grass Lick, Mrs. Edward Green, aged seventy, her son, James Green, aged twenty-one, and her twenty-six-year-old daughter, Miss Pfost, by her first husband, Francis Pfost, were murdered in cold blood, about midnight, Tuesday night, by John Morgan, a young man who had formerly been employed in the Green family who are among the prominent farmers of Jackson County. Besides killing three of the family outright, another Miss Pfost was seriously injured by a blow from the club of the fiend, but managed to escape and hide. The object of the horrible crime was to secure $56 which Morgan had learned had been received Tuesday afternoon from the sale of a horse. . .About midnight, he called at the house and arousing the family, first struck down Mrs. Green who answered his knock, and as the other members of the family rushed in, he struck the two daughters with the club he carried. Young Green ran out the door, and Morgan fearing he would escape pursued and killed him a few rods from the house. One of the daughters who was only stunned managed to escape and gave the alarm. Morgan was found in the woods, near the house, about 10 o'clock this morning. His hands and clothing were smeared with blood, and the money was on his person . . **The Wheeling Daily Intelligencer., November 4th, 1897**

The Pfost gravesite.

The funeral of Mrs. Green, formerly Mrs. Pfost, Miss Matilda Pfost, her daughter, and young James Green, her son, occurred and the three bodies were laid side by side in one grave. Marion Daily Star November 5th, 1897. Self Defense Was the Plea of Morgan

Alice Pfost, survivor and ghost.

Alice lived to the age of 75. However, for years people saw the ghost of a young woman running along Grasslick Road, and heard her cries for help. They claim it was the ghost of Alice escaping from John Morgan.

Grasslick Road where Alice's screams are heard.

Ravenswood Cemetery
2033-2965 Washington Street
Ravenswood, WV 26164
38.964556, -81.771155

Jackson County

Devil Baby

George Elwood Sharp was the son of Louis and Willa Sharp. He was born on April 27th, 1915, and passed away on July 21st, 1917. His headstone is in Ravenswood Cemetery, marking his short life and death. His picture is on the grave. Over time, the porcelain used to make the picture has begun to disintegrate, leaving what appears to be tiny horns on his head and fangs on his teeth. Still, you can hear the sound of a baby crying from the grave, and the image glows in the dark.

Old Baltimore and Ohio Tracks

The railroad entered the west side of town from what is now Sarah Lane, crossing 331

Cottageville, WV 25239
38.865233, -81.829341

Jackson County

Mysterious Echoes of Christmas Past

The B & O Railway once had a branch running from Millwood to Ripley, coursing its way through Cottageville. Now, little remains of the old tracks—except for the ghostly sound of music near Christmas.

There was once a 12.3-mile branch of railway running from Millwood to Ripley in West Virginia owned by the Baltimore and Ohio Railroad. Along the route, an elderly engineer lived in a small shack along the tracks just outside the town of Cottageville. He was well known for his love of Christmas and playing an old phonograph of Christmas music during the winter season that neighbors could hear coming from his small house.

Then one year, the music stopped playing. The old man had died. Many years would pass, and between 1965 and 1968, the railway removed the tracks and ties from the route. Along with it, they also took down the old, dilapidated shack where the engineer lived. It was not long after when the folks in the town of Cottageville began hearing the music again and seeing the ghost of the old man. It was always right before Christmastime and along the old roadbed where the track had once run. The dark silhouette of an old man would trudge along the route where the railroad once traveled until it stopped at the empty spot where the old engineer's shack once stood. The soft sound of a phonograph would slip into the air for those who stopped long enough to gape at the dark shadow sliding into view. Then the gentle lull of music and the ghost would simply disappear.

**Ghost Pond
Haunted North Bend
Rail Trail**
*Blacklick Road
New Milton, WV 26411*
1-Mile Hike:
39.279818, -80.677262
To 39.273855, -80.660171

Doddridge County

Ghost Pond on the Long Run

Old railway tracks along the Long Run.

In the 1920s, James Powell lived on a small farm along the Long Run in a sparsely settled community not far from Salem in Doddridge County. He was a widower and farmer, living alone in a small house and keeping mostly to himself except to go to Clarksburg occasionally to sell native medicinal herbs that he collected.

Two days before Christmas of 1924, three local boys, unemployed and desperate for Christmas money, broke into his home brandishing red bandanas to cover their identity. They held him at bay with a gun, rifled through his pockets, and robbed him of sixty-five dollars, a ring, and a watch. One small, cherished keepsake item remained in his pocket—a gold coin Powell had managed to secret. As it was about to be discovered, James Powell made a move to stop the thieves from taking the coin. One of the boys became enraged and shot the old man, killing him.

#4 Sherwood Tunnel along the Long Run. Among the places a ghost would walk and a man's indecipherable words were heard.

Courts later convicted the trio of murder, and police hauled the murderers away to Moundsville Prison. Powell's family laid the man to rest. His son-in-law and daughter buried his blood-stained clothing near his cabin. However, during heavy rain, the clothes were unearthed and washed into a pond nearby. Soon after, the couple reported seeing the ghostly head and neck of Powell breaking the water's surface. A great ball of fire burst from the apparition's forehead with darts shooting skyward like a Roman candle.

Rumors spread of the bizarre incident, inciting spectators to visit the site. Some would witness the ghostly form of the old man slipping up from the pond and wandering along the old train tracks running beside the Long Run stream and through the tunnels there before vanishing from sight. Those walking the railway heard voices within the tunnels, whispers described as too soft to comprehend.

Ghost Pond and nearby Tunnel #3 are on private property and must be viewed from the Rail Trail. To see them without going off-trail, you will need to take the hike in late fall and winter when the leaves are off the trees.

A reporter from the Sandusky Star Journal picked up the story in 1927 and wrote about a man who heard voices coming from the tunnel. He followed the sounds to one of the indentations in the tunnel wall called a manhole, the depressions inside the walls made so a person within the tunnel could escape if a train came down the tracks. He expected someone to be inside. He lit a match to peer within; no one was there.

The tunnel manhole—where voices are heard.

Northeastern West Virginia

Trans-Allegheny Lunatic Asylum
71 Asylum Drive
Weston, WV 26452
39.038546, -80.471726

Lewis County

Trans-Allegheny Lunatic Asylum

Also known as The Weston State Hospital and the West Virginia Hospital for the Insane, it once housed patients for many reasons. Now it holds ghosts.

The Trans-Allegheny Lunatic Asylum was a psychiatric hospital operating from 1864 until 1994. The state set up the hospital to be self-sufficient with a working farm and enough room to house 250 patients. However, at its peak in the 1950s, it had over 2,400 patients.

With the understanding of mental illness in its infancy, doctors admitted patients for such things as over-study of religion, bite of a rattlesnake, greediness, imaginary female trouble, shooting of daughter, seduction, disappointment, and kicked in the head by a horse. Alcoholism was another reason to be admitted and it appears one ghost at the asylum received some respite there for just that. Rebecca Jordan, Operations Manager at Trans-Allegheny Asylum, in an interview with Channel 13 WOWK, divulged that doctors admitted Jacob Ayers for alcoholism and delusions. And although he is not staying there anymore in human form, his ghost occasionally shows up—and he is still trying to find out who is stealing his beer!

You can bring your camera and take hundreds of pictures like I did. Then, at home, ogle-eye each searching for shadow figures and ghostly imprints of the past. Is that a shadow at the end of the hallway? Even as I stare at it for ten minutes, I can't tell. The picture gets distorted the farther back it goes!

The asylum is no longer open for patients. However, the owners offer tours and private ghost investigations. Visitors have reported laughter, crashes, booms. On one of my visits, our tour group heard low moaning outside a door where two pre-teens haunt. Strange things happen at the old asylum. Give it a try. You might see a ghost and the cost of a tour goes into the revitalization of the building.

Flinderation Tunnel
Along North Bend Rail Trail
Salem, WV 26426

Off Northwestern Pike (US 50)
There are 2 parking areas:
-**Pine Valley/Tunnel Drive**
39.290304, -80.498480
-**Flinderation Road**
39.294231, -80.509843

Harrison County

Dead People Above, Dead People Below

Flinderation Tunnel, also known as Brandy Gap Tunnel #2.

The mountains deep in West Virginia are full of old folklore, legends, and ghost stories. Many arose during the peak of the railroad, timber, and mining years when lumber and coal camps popped up along routes the trains traveled.

Those living within the camps had run-ins with spirits, and their spooky stories have been passed along from one generation to the next.

Inside the tunnel.

There is one particular place, an especially dark one, along the West Virginia North Bend Rail Trail near Salem where such a story arose. It is called Flinderation or Brandy Gap Tunnel. The tunnel was part of the Northwestern Virginia Railroad for the Baltimore and Ohio and served as a connection between Grafton and Parkersburg. Throughout the years, there have been many accounts of strange voices, sobbing, and chatter heard within the tunnel. Even when laborers were digging through the mountain from 1852 to 1857, they reported strange lights and odd sounds inside its dark recesses.

It was not easy keeping workers in this section even when the bosses scoffed at the men for being so superstitious—there was a certain amount of discontent involved with digging so close to the cemetery belonging to Enon Baptist Church settled on the hillside above the tunnel.

Some attributed the voices to the dead in that graveyard because their everlasting rest had been disturbed by all the clamor and digging below. Still, others say they came from one of their own, a worker, whose untimely death occurred on a cold winter's day in January of 1853—

Hanley died while working on the tunnel in its very early years. Fellow workers began to hear his ghostly chatter not long after. Whether they were comforted by it or felt fear, we will not know. They, too, are dead and gone. Maybe they have returned to keep their fallen comrade company. Or perhaps they simply want to keep unwary hikers away from whatever lurks just above.

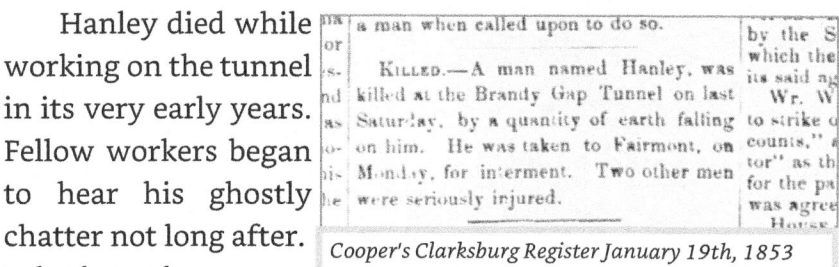

> KILLED.—A man named Hanley, was killed at the Brandy Gap Tunnel on last Saturday, by a quantity of earth falling on him. He was taken to Fairmont, on Monday, for interment. Two other men were seriously injured.

Cooper's Clarksburg Register January 19th, 1853

The dank, dark tunnel where ghosts are known to roam. And perhaps, too, a Tommyknocker or two. Legends tell that workers here heard the knock-knock-knock of Tommyknockers within these walls. Tommyknockers are moody little fairies, sometimes irritating because they were known to steal a miner's tools or food from a lunch pail, and sometimes lifesavers that also warned of rock falls with their signature knock.

Harpers Ferry, Shepherdstown, And Vicinity

West Virginia Ghost Stories, Legends, and Haunts 71

Harpers Ferry/Bolivar are historic towns at the point where the Potomac and Shenandoah rivers meet. The Appalachian Trail cuts through them. Within walking distance are shops, eateries, and enough ghost stories to sate any appetite. It is accessible on foot with paths running through Harpers Ferry National Historical Park including a Civil War Museum and period buildings such as John Brown's Fort and an old tavern.

***Harper Museum
(Harper House)***
*107 Public Way
Harpers Ferry, WV 25425
39.323077, -77.730899*

Jefferson County

The Face in the Window—Rachel Harper

Early Harpers Ferry. Image: New York Public Library.

    Harpers Ferry was initially settled with "squatter rights" by Peter Stephens, who ran a ferry service in 1732. In 1747, Robert Harper would pass through the area when building a mill for Quakers and fall in love with the area's beauty. He also saw the potential for a grist mill powered by the water where the Potomac and Shenandoah Rivers meet. He purchased the rights to the land in 1751 for a little over three-hundred dollars and, within seven months, had built a mill and improved the ferry service across the Potomac River for settlers working their way westward.

West Virginia Ghost Stories, Legends, and Haunts 73

The early ferry system at Harpers Ferry. Harpers Ferry Center Commissioned Art Collection (IMS 02846) Year: The Potomac Ferry operated from 1747-1824.

He was well-liked in the region. In fact, for those who brought grain to his mill, he ferried them across the Shenandoah or Potomac for free. He was so successful that he was able to pay off all his debts in two years. Robert's wife, Rachel, was not so enamored by the remote wilderness and the constant flooding in her small home along the rivers. Right after she came to live in the valley with her brother, who would run the mill, she and Robert built a house on the hill to avoid seasonal flooding with a grand view of the valley.

When the Revolutionary War broke out in 1775, many in the community turned away from farming to participate in the war efforts, which took a deep cut into the mill's profits. The British were also forcing the family to pay high taxes for the successful ferry business. Rachel handled the incoming cash and receipts for the ferry service. To avoid paying the taxes, she hid the money by burying it.

The Harper House in the early 1900s. To the right is a little bridge that led to a garden that legends tell holds great riches.

During normal household duties in 1780, 60-year-old Rachel fell from a ladder. She died the next day without telling anyone, even her husband, where she had buried the money. In 1782 and at age 64, Robert Harper died only a couple of years after his wife, a widower with no children. No one was ever able to find the money. Some believe Rachel hid it in the little garden across from the house. Her ghostly form, wearing the clothing of the 1700s, is seen peering in that direction from a window overlooking her garden. She is forever vigilant, guarding the cache so the tax collectors cannot find it.

The Harper House now. To the left is the garden. There is no longer a bridge running from the home to the rock wall. When walking down the street, look up to the right to the windows and watch for Rachel Harper guarding the money that many believe she hid in the garden from tax collectors.

Visitors to the home, which is now a museum, have heard bangs on the roof above. In 1775, Robert Harper's friend, Esquire Thomas Hamilton, the district magistrate who helped him draw up the land's legal issues, slipped through a rafter during the stone home's construction. He died from his injuries. His ghost still makes loud sounds on the rooftop, similar to knuckles banging on wood.

*Wager House
(next to Harper House)*
*115 Public Way
Harpers Ferry, WV 25425
39.323198, -77.730958*

Jefferson County

The Ghosts of Wager House

Harper House.

Wager House. View from High Street.

After Robert and Rachel Harper died, they willed their properties to their niece, Sarah Wager, who passed them on to her children. The Wagers built a huge house next to the older Harper home. During the Civil War, it was used as a makeshift hospital. It eventually fell into disrepair and sold to a private owner, then to the National Park Service, and renovated as a guest house for official visitors.

It was not long after the park service refurbished the house that ghost sightings began. A visitor staying in one of the rooms had just fallen to sleep. He awakened to find a man shuffling across the room carrying the limp body of another man on his shoulders. Then the two vanished as if never there. A woman in a gray hooded cloak wanders the building, holding the hand of a small girl on the stairway. And a handsome but angry man in a long coat and cane has been witnessed at the servant's stairs. He has chased a guest or two, only to disappear just as his fingers appear ready to snatch on to a shoulder.

The walkway by Harper House.

When the Wagers owned the property, they offered tenement housing to the Harper House with sublevel access. There is a small walkway running behind the houses. Park employees used these rooms while working in Harpers Ferry. One employee heard whistling in the sublevel. She raced to her car, fearing an intruder. Immediately, the young woman raised the attention of a nearby ranger who searched the home. Just as they concluded no one was there and stood in the little alley behind the home chatting, a dog rushed from the small sublevel door and knocked the ranger off his feet. After the two performed a thorough search, the animal was not found. Strangely, it was noted during the investigation that the door where the phantom dog had rushed through had been painted shut!

Camp Hill
High Street
Harpers Ferry, WV 25425
39.324527, -77.733398

Jefferson County

Camp Hill Marching Ghost Troops

The Armory, center. Image: West Virginia Regional and History Center.

When George Washington became president, he took a great interest in protecting the United States. He felt an army was needed and that army would need supplies. Instead of relying upon other countries for guns and ammunition, he began setting up permanent federal armories in the U.S.—one such arsenal was planned for the riverfront at Harpers Ferry to be called United States Armory and Arsenal at Harpers Ferry.

Some government officials objected to an armory located in Harpers Ferry, and as Washington's term was about the expire, these adversaries delayed the development. But when French privateers began pursuing American ships overseas, and war seemed on the horizon, a renewed effort to make weapons quickly in Harpers Ferry was launched.

During the building of three major components of the arsenal, a few regiments of volunteers from the United States Provisional Army under Major General Pinckney's command, still in a winter encampment on an area called Camp Hill, helped in the construction of the canal and dam. The troops would march along the street, playing their fifes and drums. Later, both Union and Confederate troops camped here. The soldiers are long gone, but their spirits are not. On still nights and if you listen closely, you can still hear the eerie echo of their feet to the ground, the call of their fifes, and a steady beat of drums.

Camp Hill served as an encampment for many troops including both Union and Confederate. At first, the armies were located in the bottomland, but because of the high amount of sickness, the men were moved to higher ground. Don't be surprised if you hear the drums of soldiers on High Street or hear the sounds of marching feet! Image: Natl. Park Service. NPS.org

My son heard it walking back to our cottage in Bolivar just up the street. It was dark, but we felt safe walking along the sidewalk with the quiet, charming cottages to our right.

West Virginia Ghost Stories, Legends, and Haunts 79

High Street, right, where soldiers would march to Camp Hill, top. Image late 1800s. Harpers Ferry Nat'l Hist'l Park Archive, Photograph No. HF-0099

He kept telling me he heard the sound of a whistle or flute following us, along with the gentle tap of footsteps. I did not know about the story and simply thought he heard the sounds inside the other cottages. The next day when one of the shopkeepers recited the story for me as I went to check out, I stood there with my mouth agape—"*Huh, what?*" I mumbled to her. Then when she explained the march of soldiers, I got goosebumps knowing he heard the ghostly procession. He had experienced what others had witnessed!

When you walk up High Street in the evening, listen for the ghost army.

Harper Cemetery
359 Fillmore Street
Harpers Ferry, WV 25425
39.323868, -77.734257

Jefferson County

Strange Goings-On at a Cemetery

Shirley Dougherty, a town storyteller/historian, once related an account about a Doctor Charles Brown who, in 1824 and upon his death, asked to be buried in the Harper Cemetery in a standing position in a casket with a glass window with his head visible above ground. After many years, the glass was broken, and the head lay exposed in the cemetery. Much to everyone's horror, a passerby caught a group of school children cutting through the cemetery and playing a rousing game of kickball with the skull! The cemetery caretaker quickly reinterred the corpse. The story lives on with accounts of a shadowy man in a top hat lurking around the stones that most believe to be the doctor.

Old Railroad Tracks
By U.S. Armory
118-198 Potomac Street
Harpers Ferry, WV 25425
39.323803, -77.730319

Jefferson County

Screaming Jenny

Image of armory, left, circa 1865 and outbuildings where Jenny lived her humble life.

The federal armory at Harpers Ferry provided full-scale production and manufacture of arms such as muskets, rifles, and pistols. There were several brick and wooden workshop buildings between the river and the town and closest to the water that the federal army had helped build.

There were also older outbuildings and sheds used to store items along the waterway.

It was not long after the Baltimore and Ohio Railway began running through Harpers Ferry near the armory in the early 1830s that the old sheds became abandoned. Those unfortunate enough to be homeless began to find shelter there. One such person was an old woman fondly called Jenny by those who watched her make her way along the river, searching for driftwood for her fire. One windy night, after tending to her fire, Jenny's dress wafted into the embers, and the hem burst into flames, quickly consuming her body. She ran frantically along the tracks and toward the river screaming for help. But in her desperate escape from the flames, Jenny did not see the evening train coming, and it smashed into her frail body, killing her. For years, train men reported seeing the old woman's ghost as a ball of fire bursting along the railway, followed by a scream as loud as the train wheels screeching across the iron rails.

The old railroad tracks where Jenny had been seen as a ball of fire bursting along the railways.

John Brown's Fort
Shenandoah Street
& Potomac Street
Harpers Ferry, WV 25425
39.323053, -77.729553

Jefferson County

John Brown's Raid on Harpers Ferry—and the Ghosts Thereafter—

John Brown's body lies
a-moldering in his grave.
John Brown's body lies
a-moldering in his grave
John Brown's body lies
a-moldering in his grave
His soul is marching on.

There is a folk song to the tune of The Battle Hymn of the Republic that began not long after abolitionist John Brown's execution. It sounds quite grisly by today's standards, but it was a popular song used by Union troops as they marched. And even if the tune's words are true and John Brown's body has decayed to nothing beneath his headstone, many believe his spirit still visits Harpers Ferry.

John Brown was raised in a deeply religious family who passionately opposed slavery. Despite his seemingly spiritual background and desire to support human rights, his antislavery tactics were radical and violent. The same man known for his heroic efforts in helping slaves escape through the Underground Railroad was also a brutal mass murderer during the stormy times before the Civil War.

On May 24th, 1856, he and seven men entered the pro-slavery town of Pottawatomie Creek. They dragged a farmer, James Doyle, and his three young sons—John-age 16, Drury-age 20, and William-age 22, from their beds in a Kansas farmhouse at midnight. James' wife, Mahala Doyle, begged for the life of her youngest son, John, who was allowed to go back into the cabin. Then, a hundred yards from the house, Brown and his sons shot down and hacked the unarmed father and sons to death. The man owned no slaves and was but a poor farmer. Brown left the wife, Mahala Doyle, a widow, and their children without a father. Two more men died that night hacked to death with swords under the same intention—to rid the frontier of slavery. The murders became known as the Pottawatomie Massacre and began a brutal guerrilla war in Kansas, and Brown became a fugitive of the law.

Brown was not portrayed so kindly by those impacted by his guerrilla tactics as in this print about the leading part Brown played in the murder of James Doyle and his sons. Image: Library of Congress Prints and Photographs.

West Virginia Ghost Stories, Legends, and Haunts   85

Brown's antislavery guerrilla warfare continued, and he fervently became more and more obsessed with what he believed was his divine right to end slavery at all costs. On the night of October 16th, 1859, 59-year-old John Brown led 21 men, including two of his sons, on a raid to seize the U.S. Arsenal at Harpers Ferry where the Shenandoah and the Potomac Rivers meet. His goal was to use the guns to create an army of former slaves that would incite a rebellion to free all slaves. His dream was to create a separate state in the Shenandoah Valley for blacks. Among his followers were both fugitive slaves and freed blacks and even some young abolitionists. There were 16 whites and five blacks with one ultimate goal in mind—to end slavery. They ranged from an 18-year-old to 44-year-old Dangerfield Newby, a fugitive slave hoping to free his wife of slavery.

Brown's men entered Harpers Ferry (rear of image) through this bridge, left, from Maryland. Image: National Park Service

While Brown began his raid, his guards, while watching the bridge, were approached by Hayward Shepherd, the station baggageman and a free person of color who came out to check on the commotion. The guards ordered him to halt, and when Shepherd turned, he was shot and killed. Image: Library of Congress

The battle within the armory. Image: National Park Service

Brown's small army invaded the city and quickly secured the federal armory and Hall's Rifle Works, a weapons manufacturer. As word got out, local militia cut off all escape routes. Then, he and his men moved along with hostages to the engine house where militia and U.S. Marines, led by Robert E. Lee, eventually captured the rebels.

Fire engine house (John Browns Fort), where hostages were kept.

The actual armory and building where the battle took place as they appeared during the raid. Image: National Park Service

During the raid, Brown's followers killed six citizens of the town, including the railroad baggage handler Hayward Shepherd, a free person of color, who came upon the men outside town. They also killed the mayor. In all, ten of Brown's died, and seven were wounded and captured.

Brown was tried and convicted of treason, then sentenced to death. His final words to the public were written in a note slipped to a reporter on his way to the gallows: *I, John Brown, am now quite certain that the crimes of this guilty land will never be purged away but with blood. I had, as I now think, vainly flattered myself that without very much bloodshed, it might be done.* He hanged on December 2nd, 1859. Mahala Doyle, whose husband and sons he had murdered in Kansas would probably say he got his just reward as John Brown's body lay a-moldering in his grave.

Execution of John Brown. Image: Library of Congress

Still, his spirit is present—some have seen his ghostly form walking the streets of Harpers Ferry as if he is still flesh and blood. In an interview with Bluefield Daily Telegraph on May 6th, 1984, Shirley Dougherty, a well-known historian on the ghosts in Harpers Ferry, noted one group of tourists who reported seeing his spirit.

They believed he was a reenactor portraying the man who tried to incite a slave rebellion and even posed for a picture with him. However, when the image was developed, the family members were quite clear. The space where the reenactor stood, on the other hand, was empty!

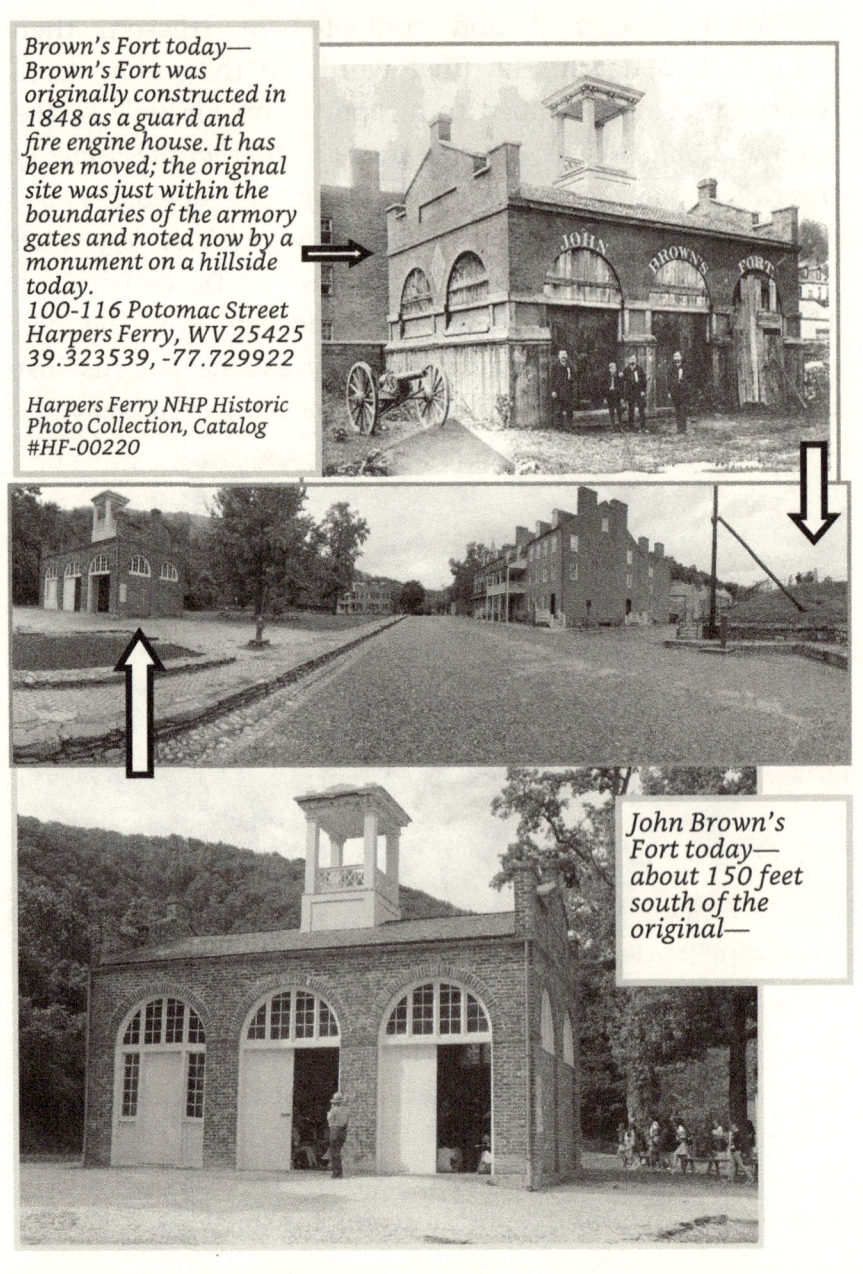

Brown's Fort today—Brown's Fort was originally constructed in 1848 as a guard and fire engine house. It has been moved; the original site was just within the boundaries of the armory gates and noted now by a monument on a hillside today.
100-116 Potomac Street Harpers Ferry, WV 25425
39.323539, -77.729922

Harpers Ferry NHP Historic Photo Collection, Catalog #HF-00220

John Brown's Fort today—about 150 feet south of the original—

Hog Alley
Harpers Ferry, WV 25425
39.323431, -77.730639

Jefferson County

Dangerfield Newby's Heroic Sacrifice to Save His Family—And His Sad Return

Dangerfield Newby

Dangerfield Newby was born into slavery, but his white father eventually freed him when he moved his family into Ohio. Dangerfield's wife, Hannah, and seven children remained slaves in Virginia. Newby was trying desperately to earn enough money to buy freedom for his wife and youngest child, who was just learning to walk. However, before Newby could obtain enough funds, he received three desperate and urgent letters from his wife stating she feared the man who enslaved her was preparing to sell her.

In the summer of 1859, and during the same time Dangerfield was frantically trying to find a way to save his wife, John Brown was making secret plans to start an insurrection. It was the same time that 44-year-old Dangerfield Newby received the final note from his wife that he kept close to himself, tucked safely in his pocket—

BRENTVILLE, August 16, 1859.

Dear Husband. your kind letter came duly to hand and it gave me much pleasure to here from you and especely to hear you are better of your rhumatism and hope when I here from you again you may be entirely well. I want you to buy me as soon as possible for if you do not get me somebody else will the servents are very disagreeable thay do all thay can to set my mistress againt me Dear Husband you not the trouble I see the last two years has ben like a trouble dream to me it is said Master is in want of monney if so I know not what time he may sell me an then all my bright hops of the futer are blasted for there has ben one bright hope to cheer me in all my troubles that is to be with you for if I thought I shoul never see you this earth would have no charms for me do all you Can for me witch I have no doubt you will I want to see you so much the Chrildren are all well the baby cannot walk yet all it can step around enny thing by holding on it is very much like Agnes I mus bring my letter to Close as I have no newes to write you mus write soon and say when you think you Can Come.

Your affectionate Wife HARRIET NEWBY.

The U.S. Marines storming the engine house—Insurgents firing through holes in the doors. Image: Library of Congress.

Desperate to free his family, Newby joined John Brown's raid at Harpers Ferry. Low on ammunition during the attack, local townspeople resorted to using whatever they could jam into their gun barrels. One was shooting six-inch spikes, which met its mark on Newby's neck and killed him.

Outraged at the assault on their town, citizens later took Newby's body, repeatedly stabbed it, and amputated the limbs. His body was then tossed into the alley to be eaten by hogs running the streets. But not before the simple note from his wife begging for his help was found within his pocket.

Hog Alley, where witnesses have seen the ghost of a man who tried in vain to save his family.

The alley, today, is called Hog Alley. Pedestrians have witnessed Dangerfield Newby's ghost walking near this off-street wearing baggy pants and a slouch hat. He dons a horrible scar across his throat and appears to be focused hard upon the ground as if he is still trying desperately to find a way to free his wife and child.

Maryland Heights

As seen from the footbridge or The Point (the tip of Harpers Ferry near the footbridge over the river)
39.322986, -77.728587
Or take the rigorous trail to Maryland Heights
Trailhead: 39.329084, -77.731310

Jefferson County

Little Campfire Lights at Maryland Heights

Maryland Heights.

The Point.

In May of 1862, Union Troops built a defense on Maryland Heights, the highest mountain overlooking the town of Harpers Ferry. It would become the grounds for the first battle between Union and Confederate troops in Maryland (September 12th-15th, 1862).

The battle on the mountain lasted nine hours, beginning at 6:30 a.m. on September 13th, 1862, and ended with the Confederacy forcing the Union troops to abandon their position on Maryland Heights and descend into Harpers Ferry. As part of the Harpers Ferry Battle, the Confederate Army had 39 killed. The Union had 44 killed, many dying on the mountain.

The land around the battlefield is, for the most part, quiet now. However, hikers on the Maryland Heights trail where the soldiers battled have watched with fascination as a soldier or two shows up on the path. Believing them to be either reenactors or ardent Civil War buffs, they are stunned when the figures completely vanish. An occasional gunshot rings out in the air, and twinkling lights, perhaps from a ghostly lantern or fire, have been known to catch the eye.

Maryland Heights trail, a rigorous climb.

Soldiers at Harpers Ferry/Maryland Heights.

You can get a spectacular view of Harpers Ferry from Maryland Heights and perhaps, if lucky, you will see a ghost!

A view of Maryland Heights from the tip of Harpers Ferry called The Point.

If you get a chance at dusk, wander to The Point, the jutting of land at the tip of Harpers Ferry by the bridge crossing to Maryland and near John Brown's Fort. During the evening, as darkness sets over the town, some have heard ghostly guns across the river and caught the flicker of spectral campfires on the mountainside.

Town House
High Street
Harpers Ferry, WV 25425
39.323844, -77.731615

Jefferson County

Ghost of the Drummer Boy

A Confederate drummer boy, circa 1861 and Town House.

During the Civil War, many of the buildings in Harpers Ferry housed soldiers. One stone house was occupied by Union soldiers who captured a Confederate drummer boy and used him as a servant to take care of their cleaning and chores. The boy missed home and constantly cried, begging the men to return him to his ma. One night, the men were drunk and intolerant. They began to bully the boy and toss him around the room, pretending to throw him out the window. One soldier missed his catch, and the boy fell from his grasp and out on to the street. He died instantly. Since that time, people have heard the sounds of the boy begging to go home to his ma along with his cries and snuffles.

Old Iron Horse Inn
151 Potomac Street
Harpers Ferry, WV 25425
39.324469, -77.732058

Jefferson County

Ghost of a Soldier Spy

Old Iron Horse Inn.

The Iron Horse Inn, circa 1798, was once owned by Harpers Ferry's earliest ghost storyteller, Shirley Dougherty. Upon moving in, she and her family noticed a door on the upper floor would shake violently following the banging sound of what appeared to be someone falling down the stairs.

An older man living in the community knew the history of the building. He told her that during the Civil War and right before a battle, an officer sent an inexperienced Confederate soldier across the river to spy on the Union troops. While he was walking near the home on Potomac Street, he was questioned and, in fear, panicked. The soldier dashed into the house and rushed up the stairs to hide. Just as he opened a doorway at the top of the stairs, an officer who had been watching from the window shot the young Confederate soldier point blank, sending him crashing down the staircase. Now, his ghost comes back once in a while to relive the horrible moment he died—in a shudder of doors and a bang and crash down the steps.

Brick Building
31 High Street
Harpers Ferry, WV 25425
39.323211, -77.730667

Jefferson County

Crying Baby

Legends say that if you stand on the stone steps, you can hear a babe's cries.

People often comment that they hear a baby's cries on the third floor of the brick building just to the right of the historic stone steps. In a 1989 Washington Post article about the ghost tours in Harpers Ferry, a young woman reported that on a walking tour, the group scattered in a panic after hearing the baby's cries while standing outside listening to the guide talk about the ghostly history.

During the siege of Harpers Ferry, a baby was killed by the shelling in the vicinity of the building, as told in the memoirs of Annie Marmion, who was eight-years-old and living near the building during the battle. Its soft whimpers have lingered, a ghostly reminder of the horrors that even impacted civilians during the Civil War.

In Under Fire, Annie P. Marmion, then an 8 year-old, resided in Marmion Hall (tenement homes along Public Way next to the Harper House as seen in the upper part of the picture) with her family during the entire conflict.

They were just above this brick building, front. Her father was a doctor and stayed to attend those who did not leave. She writes this in her memoirs and it is believed to be the ghost baby—"houses are destroyed in various parts of the town; in one the shell first kills an infant in its mother's arms, then wounds the mother..."

Image: Harpers Ferry National Historical Park (after restoration of buildings)

St. Peter's Roman Catholic Church
110 Church Street
Harpers Ferry, WV 25425
39.322817, -77.731157

Jefferson County

Father Michael Stays Behind

St. Peter's Catholic Church has been a powerful icon above Harpers Ferry since its completion in 1833. There is no doubt the deeds of those who worked inside its walls were just as prominent. One such person was Father Michael Costello, the priest at St. Peter's from 1857 to 1867. He would find himself in the center of battle when he was only 28 years old, not only during the raid by John Brown but later when he stayed in the city during the Civil War. It is the only church in Harpers Ferry that remained after the war, an achievement credited to Father Costello. When the town would come under fire, he flew a Union Jack flag above the church to show neutrality.

Father Costello. Image: NPS.org

Father Costello would watch the battles play out from atop the hill and under fire. During the raid by John Brown, he was allowed to attend a dying man, giving him last rites—his story is told through a letter sent to Father Harrington, at All Hallows College—

...I suppose you have heard about the invasion made by Northern abolitionists to liberate the slaves of Virginia, and as an account from me may not prove uninteresting to you, I shall give you a short sketch of it.

On the night of the 16th of October last, a party of abolitionists came to Harper's Ferry, and while the citizens peacefully slept, they took possession of the United States' Armoury, Rifle Works, and Arsenal. Next morning, when the inhabitants awoke, they were surprised to see parties of armed men patrolling the streets, and as some of them attempted to pass to their employment they were taken prisoners by the insurgents and marched into the Armoury, where they were placed under guard. As soon as the object of the insurrection became known, the citizens prepared to defend themselves and drive away the invaders. Accordingly, armed with any old guns they could find, they shot at the enemy who appeared in the streets, and the invaders returning their fire mortally wounded one of the citizens. The wounded man being a Catholic, I was called to attend him, and as I had to pass through the insurgents on my way, when I started I had very little hope that they would allow me to pass, as they were making prisoners of all they could catch. However, they allowed me to attend the dying man. I administered to him the last Sacraments, and he died soon after. During the day volunteer companies came from every direction to the aid of the inhabitants, and the firing continued without intermission, several of the invaders and four of the citizens losing their lives. At night, I attended another member of my congregation who was dangerously wounded. Meantime a company of the United States' soldiers arrived from Washington, and were immediately drawn up in front of the engine-house, into which "Osswattomie" Browne and his followers with their prisoners were finally driven. . . Michael A Costello, Letter to Father Harrington, All Hallows College, February 11th, 1860, Archives of the Roman Catholic Diocese of Richmond. Transcribed by Christopher C. Fennell

It is no surprise that such allegiances would leave their mark on the land and the church. Visitors walking up the stone steps, past the church, and along the Appalachian Trail to Jefferson Rock have seen the image of a man in a friar hat making his way along the walkway. There has also been a priestly figure who appears to be focusing hard on a book before he turns along the northern exterior and vanishes right into the stone wall, most likely a door before church refurbishments. There is no doubt that it is the heroic priest who was given a chance to go back to Ireland during the war but refrained in order to stay with the war-scarred people of his parish. He passed away only two years after the war ended and at only age 34.

But there is one more ghost whose story should be told here. It is that of a wounded soldier during the battle at Harpers Ferry. Father Costello carried on with services and pastoral duties throughout the battles, even though soldiers used the church and the school as makeshift hospitals. He provided spiritual support to those soldiers who were wounded or dying. One such soldier lay on the church's lawn, mortally wounded but waiting for the doctor to see him. As the blood drained from his body, stretcher-bearers finally carried him inside. Those around him heard his guttural whisper just as he came through the threshold of the church: *Thank God, I am saved.* To this day, visitors standing near the church can hear those very words the soldier whispered just before he died.

Bolivar Heights Battlefield
Whitman Avenue
Bolivar, WV 25425
39.322560, -77.761399

Jefferson County

Phantom Soldiers of Battle of Bolivar Heights

Bolivar Heights Battlefield.

On April 8th, 1861, Virginia Militia stood atop the hills of Bolivar, readying to seize Harpers Ferry. Thousands of Virginia Militia were camped here for training throughout the summer. Then on October 16th, 1861, 500 Confederate soldiers battled 600 Union soldiers on the ridge. Five men died before the Confederates retreated. In the still of the night on October evenings, when the air is thick, and the traffic has lulled, you can hear the echo of phantom soldiers and ghostly guns. Those passing by before you have listened to the unearthly sounds of soldiers riding the wind—from the noise of everyday camp life to the roar of battle.

Hilltop House Hotel and Overlook
400 E Ridge Street
Harpers Ferry, WV 25425
39.326204, -77.736318

Jefferson County

Banging Pots

Hilltop House Hotel.

The Hilltop Hotel is settled on a cliff overlooking both the Potomac and the Shenandoah rivers. Thomas S. Lovett originally built the hotel in 1888; it was destroyed and rebuilt after two fires, one in 1912 and one in 1919. It has ghosts, albeit none from a fire. When the hotel was still in operation, visitors and staff, alike, would hear the banging of pots and dishes, laughter, and voices. Ghostly soldiers are seen on the property, remnants before the hotel was built and during the Civil War.

The Point at the Rivers
Also the Original Site of Robert Harpers Ferry
Harpers Ferry, WV 25425
39.323278, -77.728578

To access, you can walk behind the National Park Service buildings on Shenandoah Street. There is a trail along the bank.

Jefferson County

The Dead Peddler's Warning

The Point.

A figure wearing a red shirt and baggy trousers has occasionally rushed up from the Potomac and warned townspeople when there is an emergency, like someone drowning when the river rises. He has hailed more than a few people before disappearing into a mist.

Old-timers explain his story as this—

Sixty-nine-year-old Moses Fine was a Russian immigrant and a peddler. He had resided in the communities of Bolivar and Harpers Ferry for at least thirty-five years, living on Shenandoah Street in Harpers Ferry in the 1920s and selling his wares throughout the countryside. He was well-liked and trusted among those in the outlying area where he sold his wares. Moses was killed by a speeding, drunk driver on August 20th, 1923. Not long after, his ghost began showing up to warn others before horrifying accidents happened to them.

John Brown Farmhouse Headquarters—Kennedy House
The John Brown Historical Foundation
2406 Chestnut Grove Road
Sharpsburg, MD 21782
39.380171, -77.715885

Washington County, MD

Ghosts of the Lost Raid

The Kennedy Farmhouse where John Brown and his supporters stayed before the raid. Image: NPS.org

Before the raid on Harpers Ferry to incite a slave rebellion, John Brown, under the name Isaac Smith, rented this farm in 1859 for three months and $35 in gold while he planned his battle and gathered his men. Before the raid, the men slept in the attic. Much of the paranormal activity seems to collect here. There are the sounds of footsteps, snorting, snoring, and chatter. On the stairway, a ghostly crowd of men head upstairs for sleep before the battle.

Antietam National Battlefield
*Battle of Antietam
(Battle of Sharpsburg)
5831 Dunker Church Road
Sharpsburg, MD 21782
39.470017, -77.740000*

Washington County, MD

Bloody Lane

Fought along the farmland around Antietam Creek near Sharpsburg, Maryland, the Battle of Antietam is considered one of the Civil War's bloodiest battles. On September 17th, 1862, General Robert E. Lee and General George McClellan came face to face at the first battle on northern soil. Four hours of intense fighting occurred on an old sunken road between two farms.

Confederate soldiers retreated, but not before bodies piled up in agonizing numbers in that road. Over 3,675 men lost their lives. General Lee withdrew across the river on September 18th, with 10,318 casualties (of 38,000 engaged) to General McClellan's 12,401 (of 75,000).

Bloody Lane on right wing, where a large number of soldiers were killed at the Battle of Antietam. Image: Library of Congress.

It is humbling to walk the dirt path called Bloody Lane, knowing how many died there, who gave their lives for others' freedom. Because this was one big decisive battle—it allowed President Lincoln to issue the Emancipation Proclamation on January 1st, 1863, which freed the slaves still held in the South. The proclamation declared: "that all persons held as slaves" within the rebellious states "are, and henceforward shall be free." It is not surprising, in the least, to hear that people have seen the ghostly apparitions of soldiers walking the fields nearby the battlefield. The scent of ghostly gunpowder wafts to nostrils, and a blue ball of light flashes across the old fields. There is a certain heavy energy in the air following those who stroll the trails.

Bloody Lane today.

McDonogh School in Owings Mills is a private school in Maryland. On September 17th, 1982, a class from the school took a field trip to mark the 120th anniversary of the battle. A part of their assignment during the trip was, at sunset, to walk the path of Bloody Lane with eyes closed and lay down to take in the magnitude of the battle story told to them ahead of time by two teachers dressed in soldier's uniforms.

The students did as instructed, but the two teachers decided to play a cruel prank on the kids and run through the field with blankets to frighten them during the lesson. Their joke came to an abrupt halt when one of the teachers was caught in barbed wire partway to the children and moaned loudly in pain. Some of the students heard the sound and were terrified, believing it was a dead soldier rising and began to scream.

As the teachers detached the wire and made their way to the students to calm them and let them know they were only playing a practical joke, they were the ones who were shocked. Some of the students had actually seen a ghostly riderless horse jumping over them while they lay there!

Several students were sure they heard what sounded like men belting out the Christmas song *Deck the Halls*, the particular words "Fa-la-la-la-la, la-la-la-la" filling the air, but later believed to be a spectral battle cry of the long-dead soldiers of the Irish Brigade yelling out "Faugh A Ballagh," meaning "Clear the way!"

Years ago, a group of Civil War reenactors decided to set up camp along Bloody Lane. After they had laid down for sleep, they began to hear low moans and groans sometime during the night. Unsettled, each individually made their way back to their cars to finish out the night until one lone reenactor remained behind. Suddenly, a scream filled the air, and the men in their vehicles jumped out to find the only man left behind rushing from the camp thoroughly shaken. When the reenactor could finally catch his breath, he told the men that while he lay there half-awake, he had seen a hand and arm raise from the earth beneath him, slide across his chest and pull him as if to drag him down into the packed dirt. When he screamed, the hand and arm vanished!

Burnside's Bridge (Lower Bridge)
18125 Old Burnside's Bridge Road
Sharpsburg, MD 21782
39.449700, -77.732477

Washington County, MD

Eerie Blue Balls of Light

Burnside's Bridge.
Image: Library of Congress.

During the Battle of Antietam, General Ambrose Burnside spent hours attempting to get his Union soldiers across a stone bridge over Antietam Creek. They succeeded. At this bridge, called Burnside's Bridge, visitors have sighted blue balls of light moving in the darkness. According to a couple who recently visited the site and got a startling peek into the past, you can hear the *pat-pat-pat* of a distant drum making a steady beat before going completely silent.

Battle of Shepherdstown
4389 River Road
Shepherdstown, WV 25443
Parking for trail:
39.426995, -77.783471

Jefferson County

Little Coin Left by a Ghost

Boteler's Ford, Potomac River near Shepherdstown. Point at which Confederate Army crossed after the Battle of Antietam with the Federal Army hot in pursuit.

Forty-eight hours after being beaten in The Battle of Antietam, Confederate General Robert E. Lee decided to retreat with his troops. They would find safety in Virginia by crossing the Potomac River at Boteler's Ford, a principal crossing point a mile and a half downstream from Shepherdstown.

Boteler's Ford —Point at which Confederate Army crossed. Image from 1861-1865. Library of Congress.

But the campaign for both sides was continuing, so Union troops were hot on their heels in pursuit when the Confederates attempted to cross the river. There were several skirmishes, and the Confederates came out victors. Still, the battle would end the Campaign of Maryland for Lee when the Union drove his troops out of Maryland.

Boteler's Ford today in the center of the picture. The riverbank can be accessed by a trail that follows past an old cement factory where troops were held. The ford was used for the Army of Northern Virginia to escape, but was also used by earlier settlers to cross the wide river. Then, it was called Pack Horse Ford.

You can walk the trails and look out on the Potomac and see the ford where General Lee sat on horseback watching his troops file through before the battle ensued. You can take in the old cement factory where these fighting men hid behind the stone walls to keep from getting shot. The battle lasted only four hours. There were 73 Union soldiers killed and 36 Confederate soldiers who lost their lives.

The battlefield is eerily quiet. We heard the hushed sound of voices on the trail and even after a thorough search, could not trace the origin.

It was not until November 17th, 2016, that the Civil War Trust purchased 11 acres of land on the 1862 Battle of Shepherdstown. It is a place to explore old things about the Civil War and new things about the spirits remaining. Listen closely. You may hear the cries of men long gone, hear the drums and the guns and the splash of horse hooves as they cross the ford. Or you might feel a strange sensation that you are being watched while you walk the path along the river. I did. When I turned, I saw a shadow standing next to a tree. I walked over to investigate, thinking that surely it was just the shadows on a sunny day wiggling through the canopy of leaves. But at my feet, I found a coin. I reached down to pick it up and turned it over in my fingers. It was so old that I could not decipher anything on it. It almost killed me, but knowing it was a historical site, I had to let that little coin go. I put it down next to the tree and left it there for the ghost.

The Entler Hotel
Shepherdstown Museum
129 E German Street
Shepherdstown, WV 25443
39.430488, -77.804417

Jefferson County

Ghost of Peyton Smith at the Old Globe Tavern

Shepherdstown Museum.

The Shepherdstown Museum was once the building that housed the Entler Hotel providing lodging and Globe Tavern, offering drinks and entertainment. On a Tuesday in November 1809, 17-year-old Peyton Bull Smith and 16-year-old Joseph Holmes had been drinking and playing cards.

Smith had just graduated in 1808 from William and Mary College in Williamsburg, Virginia, and had just set up an office with Holmes, his boyhood friend. The two disagreed about a trivial matter during the game, and Smith called Holmes "a damned fool."

Spurred on with taunts by some military recruiting officers at the table, Holmes unwillingly challenged Smith to a duel. Smith accepted, and the two made arrangements to fight in a duel at daybreak on the Maryland side of the Potomac River. It was Tuesday, November 28th, 1809.

Peyton Smith was a great shooter. Holmes was not so good and was considered doomed. But when arbitrators marked the distance and the men stood erect and raised their pistols, Holmes would fire, and his shot would hit its mark. Smith did not fire his gun.

Smith was carried to Entler Hotel and laid in an upstairs room. A servant had been sent earlier to warn the man's mother of the duel that was going to take place. She rushed to the scene but only made it just to hear her son's last breaths. Peyton Smith died in just a few hours.

> *FATAL DUEL-With the most painful sensations we announce the death of Mr. Peyton Bull Smith, eldest son of General John Smith of this County, Representative in Congress. In the death of this young gentleman we have again to deplore the prevalence of a practice which by rapid strides has gained uncontrolled ascendancy throughout the civilized world. He fell a victim in a duel with Mr. Joseph Holmes of this place, on Tuesday last, near Shepherdstown, on the Maryland side of the Potomac . . .* **The Gazette. Winchester December 1st, 1809**

Over the years, those walking within the walls of the building have heard footsteps and moans. Most believe it is the ghost of Peyton Smith whose voice calls out. The sound of furniture moving resounds against the walls, perhaps spirits of those preparing the room for the heroic young man who refused to shoot his childhood friend.

Jefferson Security Bank
AKA Yellow Brick Road Restaurant
201 E German Street
Shepherdstown, WV 25443
39.430421, -77.804111

Jefferson County

The Ghost at Table 25

There is something about the old yellow brick building on the corner in Shepherdstown. In 1906, lot owners razed the brick building to erect the Jefferson Security Bank; then, after 69 years in business, new owners turned the structure into a restaurant around 1975. Following its conversion into a restaurant, strange things began to happen. Glasses randomly fell off shelves, and people got a strange, ghostly sensation around Table 25.

Shepherdstown Sweet Shop & Bakery
100 W German Street
Shepherdstown, WV 25443
39.430782, -77.806070

Jefferson County

Ghosts of an Old Battlefield Hospital

Moulder Hall was used as an emergency hospital after the Battle of Antietam.

The building on the corner of German Street and King Street was a general store from the early 1800s to the 1980s. It was also a makeshift hospital during the Civil War. Soldiers wounded in the Battle of Antietam, September 17th, 1862, were taken to this building, second floor, for emergency surgery.

As a hospital, the rooms were crowded with the wounded and their groans and cries. Now, the building is the Shepherdstown Sweet Shop Bakery with delicious pastries and cookies. (Yes, I could not help but stop in and try a home-baked cookie, and it was *to die for*). Bakery workers have reported a Civil War soldier's ghostly form and have felt a mysterious presence brush past as they bake. The sound of mumbling and groans drift from somewhere above the pastry shop, old remnants from its history as a Civil War hospital. Every few years, workers digging on nearby properties discover bones believed to be that of soldiers who had limbs amputated, and the remains tossed from upper windows so that laborers could load them in wagons and cart away.

McMurran Hall
S King Street
Shepherdstown, WV 25443
39.431047, -77.805463

Jefferson County

Old Man in the Clock Tower

The building served as the Jefferson County Courthouse right after the Civil War. The clock in the tower was originally in an old Episcopal Church but moved to the building in 1860. It eventually became the first building for Shepherdstown University in 1871. It has a ghost—an old man will peer out of the shutters at the students walking past at night. Some believe it might be a soldier. Like so many other buildings in this small town, medical personnel used the structure as a hospital during the Civil War.

The Entler-Weltzheimer House
E High Street
Shepherdstown, WV 25443
39.431959, -77.804610

Jefferson County

The Dead Cobbler

Some who walk along East High Street in Shepherdstown hear incessant *tap-tap-tapping*. It lasts for only a few moments while they pass a small wooden 18th century home, then fades away. It is quite a mystery to those who pause in their steps, nosing around the sidewalk.

They search to find the source before walking away none-the-wiser for all their investigating.

There are few alive today that recall the source for such a mysterious sound. But some might remember that the little home called the Weltzheimer House was once rented to George Yontz, a much-loved shoe cobbler. On December 3rd, 1910, customers stopping into his shop did not receive an answer when they knocked on the door. When authorities could finally enter, they found 68-year-old George dead and lying on the floor.

For a while, all was quiet along the street. Then not long after he died, those who walked near his house at night could hear the *tap-tap-tapping* of the hammer to the shoe again. You may be able to listen to it, too, with a short walk along East High Street where the old dead cobbler's shop still stands.

New Street
Shepherdstown, WV 25443
39.430607, -77.808441

Jefferson County

The Ghost of Susie Ferrell

It was near the front porch steps where a killer shot a young woman and her ghost walks the street outside. Image: Historic Shepherdstown.

Harry Smootz told railroad employee Fillmore Reynolds that if he could not have pretty Shepherdstown native Susie Ferrell, he would most certainly kill her. The two were riding together in a caboose heading toward Hagerstown.

Although Susie was just an acquaintance, he was quite smitten with her. He had asked her to marry him. She had refused. Reynolds chuckled awkwardly and swallowed hard, waiting for Smootz to laugh and say he was kidding. He did not. Still, Reynolds tossed aside the strange confession as nothing more than a hollow threat like several others to whom Smootz had confessed his intentions. Then he began to stalk her, constantly walking in front of her house and following her to her friends' homes.

On the evening of January 21st, 1892, while two friends, 21-year-old Lucy Schoppert and 23-year-old Susie Ferrell, were heading along New Street toward the local sledding hill around 6:45 p.m., the young women were stopped by Harry Smootz hailing them. Smootz slipped down from King Street and grabbed Ferrell around the neck with his left arm, and waved a revolver at her in his right. He had pressed her face against his breast. As her friend called desperately for help, Susie struggled. Another young man, Harry Staley, came forward, and Smootz threatened to shoot Susie. Staley stepped back and started to shout, "Murder!" Then, the shot rang out. The bullet entered the young woman's skull and penetrated the brain. Smootz dropped her and ran; then, someone carried Susie into Reverend Neel's home. She died almost immediately.

Smootz pleaded insanity. But he was convicted of first-degree murder. The judge sentenced him to hang on October 7th, 1892. However, he never made it to the noose. On the morning of September 21st, 1892, Smootz was discovered in his jail cell dead. He died from an overdose of morphine.

No one seems to know how he came to get the morphine. We do know, however, that people believe the young woman haunts New Street. She walks along the sidewalk as if still waiting for the sled ride on that fateful night. Then, she vanishes from sight.

Southeastern West Virginia

Big Bend Tunnel
John Henry Historical Park
3262 WV-3
Talcott, WV 25951
37.649686, -80.766524

Summers County

The Legend of John Henry

Construction of Big Bend (aka Great Bend) Tunnel—Where John Henry defeated the steam drill. Image: Library of Congress.

The legend of John Henry has been passed down in folk songs, many books, and even an animated Disney cartoon.

John Henry, a freed slave, worked for the railroad. He was a giant of a man for his time in the 1870s—six feet tall and two-hundred pounds. In fact, as legends tell he was nearly forty pounds when he was born and stood up bawling for his milk only hours after birth. Most believe he was from Virginia and an African America freshly freed from slavery.

The tunnel today.

He was what they once called a steel-driving man. His job was among the thousands of men and boys who the Chesapeake and Ohio Railroad Company paid to hammer steel stakes into the nearly impassable red shale walls of mountains as the railway pushed westward. The holes they drove into the walls were filled with explosives. Teams would blast out cavities so the men could go deeper, paving the way for tunnels for the trains to pass through.

When the steam powered hammer was invented, the railway companies were eager to adopt this new tool. It saved both time and money as they did not need to hire as many workers. John Henry challenged the machine's ability to work better than hired men in a competition—the building of a mile long mountain tunnel in West Virginia.

A contest was held. A machine was set up on one side of the railroad track and John Henry stood on the other holding a twenty pound hammer with the head greased in tallow. The steam drill could not keep up. John Henry drove the steel for thirty minutes to the chants of his fellow steel drivers yelling: *Swing, man, swing*! And when he was finished, he had two seven-foot holes. The drilling machine only had one hole that was nine feet deep. John Henry won, only to die from exhaustion soon after.

Inside the tunnel.

The tunnel, right.

It took three years to build the tunnel called Great Bend. But it was only weeks after the competition that the workers began to hear the ghostly ringing sounds of John Henry's hammer still driving stakes within. It nearly stopped the work on the tunnel. As much as their lead supervisor tried to convince the laborers it was water leaking from the roof, few believed him. It was his ghost. Legends still exist that John Henry's ghost lingers on at Great Bend Tunnel near Talcott, West Virginia where the contest was held. A large statue has also been erected in a park there to commemorate the event. You can hear him still hammering away within if you listen closely. You can listen to the ghostly chants of the other workmen encouraging him to win.

Site of Morris Massacre
13523 Turnpike Road
Summersville, WV 26651
38.256736, -81.028427

Nicholas County

The Morris Massacre

Henry Morris and his wife, Mary, lived with seven daughters and a son along Peters Creek in the late 1700s. Henry had a favorite bear hunting dog he called Watch that he kept by his side for protection from the Native Indians that were known to attack settlers in the area. The dog's nose was so keen that he could catch the scent of prey or enemy from quite some distance. Watch's hackles would rise and warn Henry.

In the fall of 1791, a raggedy man in buckskins who called himself Mister Allen asked to board at Henry's home for the winter. Henry befriended the man, even though Watch's hackles would rise whenever he was around the lodger. The two hunted together for the winter.

The next spring, Henry headed to Fort Clendenin and mentioned this Mister Allen, who he had befriended. Someone said that his newfound buddy was, most likely, Simon Girty, an unscrupulous man who sided with the Native Indians. His reputation for torturing and killing settlers was well known. A deep scar along his forehead was the easiest way to disclose his true identity. Upon his return, Henry confronted his hunting companion, and the man denied being Girty. But Henry reached out and pushed back the hair, and sure enough, there was a deep scar across his forehead. It was none other than Simon Girty. Henry told Girty he had to leave, and when he did, Girty called out to Henry's hunting dog and bade him follow him into the woods. Two of Henry's children, 14-year-old Betsy and 12-year-old Margaret "Peggy," called the dog back. It angered Girty. He threatened to get them back, but he left, and all seemed well.

Three weeks after the incident, Henry returned from a hunt, and his dog began to act strangely. He hurried to his home and noted two of his daughters were missing. They had gone to the field to collect up the calves for the night. Fear seeped through Henry when he went out into the yard. He knew something was wrong even before he heard the horrible scream. He ran in the direction and came across his daughter, Peggy. She had been tomahawked, scalped, and someone had broken her back, but she had almost managed to escape. She probably would have outrun her attackers completely if not for tripping over a grapevine.

Betsy was scalped and stabbed four times with a butcher knife so hard each thrust had gone entirely through her tiny body. Peggy would die before morning light, but not before she identified Simon Girty and said her final words: "Father, I am killed." Henry's winter hunting companion was the murderer.

The field where the girls were murdered and where the tiny cemetery is located. Burial at: Lockwood Field-Fairview Baptist Church Cemetery—38.256725, -81.028414.

The two girls were buried side by side in a grave not far from the roadway. If you visit, stand by the highway, and it is not difficult to imagine the sound of the girls' ghostly wails on the wind and the howl of Henry's dog, Watch, baying in warning to the man who would not heed the caution of his hackles rising at the sight of old Simon Girty.

Laurel Creek Ford by Panther Mountain
WV-129
Summersville, WV 26651
Bethel Church: 38.252472, -80.965925
The Ford: 38.252081, -80.968602

Nicholas County

Ghost Dog of Laurel Creek Ford

Where the story begins—Laurel Creek is behind the Bethel United Methodist Church, center, in the copse of trees and where a group of Tipton teens were heading back home after a church meeting and ran into the Ghost at the Ford.

In the shadows of Panther Mountain, Laurel Creek makes a lazy meander beneath a tunnel of thick trees in a cozy, little glen that parallels the road, WV-129. Near the location, the pretty, poplar-sided Bethel United Methodist Church has been standing since 1868. Once there was a ford over Laurel Creek in the roadway for carriages and close by, a handrail and bridge for pedestrian traffic.

Around 1873, an old Syrian pushcart peddler selling notions and goods and his beloved, blood-red collie were murdered along this little creek and by the ford. A thief had robbed the poor man of his wares and his money. Both the dog's throat and the peddler's throat were slit from ear to ear. It was not long before folks who traveled along the creek and roadway began to see the most horrifying sight—that of a glowing red dog that walked three feet above the ground. It was not so bad that the dog would show up in its eerie glow, but it would follow travelers along the creek until it stopped just short of the ford and disappear!

Laurel Creek where the ghostly dog belonging to the murdered peddler followed those heading toward the ford.

In the Sunday Charleston Gazette, March 29th, 1953 article called Ghost at the Ford, Lonnie Legge related a story passed down to him by his father of a group of teens from Tipton who had attended a social church function at the old Bethel Church about a mile and a half away. Lonnie Legge's father began the story by saying this: "There was a protracted meeting going on at Bethel Church, and a bunch of us boys and girls from Tipton, three miles below the church, decided to attend. Going meant a walk of about six miles, but boys and girls didn't regard a little hike like that as anything of a hindrance to courtship—"

However, on one particular night, when the boys and girls walked home after attending the church, they teased each other about wanting to see the ghost of the peddler along the creek. Of course, the boys wanted to show their bravery to the girls, but they soon found out that perhaps too much challenging and talk might sabotage future night wooing possibilities.

—After meeting, the crowd left the church on their return trip in high spirits. One young fellow, Charlie, I think his name was, was particularly brave. "If that infernal dog tries to follow me, I'm going to tie a knot in his tail."

The storm that had threatened earlier was approaching fast with flash after flash of lightning and crashing thunder that made the hills themselves shudder. In the dim tunnel at the ford, the lightning flashes gave everything an eerie, unreal appearance. The person walking beside you looked like a walking corpse.

Close to the creek everyone in the crowd heard an exclamation from Charley, who was walking in the rear with his girl. Looking back, they all saw a large red dog trotting along in the air beside him. Charley must have had plenty of nerve because, even as they looked, he reached out with both hands to grab it, but he said afterwards "Never even touched it." Just then hell itself seemed to break loose. The apparition whirled over on its back with fire and smoke flying out of its nose and mouth in twin streams and the smell of the air was like being close to where lightning had struck. No one took time to use the footlog across the ford. Girls and boys alike splashed through the water and didn't slow down until they were out of breath and about a quarter mile downstream. After counting noses, they discovered everyone was present except Charlie. Poor old Charlie. Either the ghost had gotten him or in the headlong rush, he had fallen and broken his neck. Just then someone called from up ahead. It was Charlie. "Come on! I'm still out in front!" When the rest of the crowd caught up with him the smell of lightning still was strong about him--Charleston Gazette March 29, 1953. Lonnie E. Legge

It is not difficult to imagine the dark tunnel of trees that once encompassed the little creek and how scary it would be to walk through them.

Such, the boys spent much time afterward relenting they had talked up the ghost because the girls refused to go past that dark spot over the ford again. However, you may someday pass along the little Laurel Creek tucked into the hollow of Panther Mountain. When you do, keep your eyes on the road as not to catch the attention of the ghostly apparition of a blood-red dog at the place of the old ford because others have. And certainly, do not challenge him, or you just might get the surprise of your life just like those young folks did walking home from church!

Where the ford once stood not far from Bethel United Methodist Church.

Peter's Creek Valley
Along WV-39 Turnpike Road
Summersville, WV 26651
38.259538, -81.034756 to
38.265306, -81.012448

Nicholas County

Haunted Hollow— Ghost left behind from the Skirmish in Summersville

A ghost of a Union soldier, barely out of his youth, wanders the deep hollow along Peters Creek in Nicholas County. The soldier's pained moaning along with his loyal dog's sad whine echoes with the wind flowing in the deep hollow between the roadway and the water's edge. This ghost can blame his demise on a certain Rebel spy who also drifted through the area. Her name was Nancy Hart. Although his death was not physically caused by her hands, it was an inadvertent result of Nancy's actions.

Nancy had grown up on a family farm in West Virginia and learned at a young age how to shoot guns and pistols and handle a horse. She lived there until the Civil War broke out, then having great compassion for the southern cause, moved in with her sister's family, Mary and William Price. At the time, she was around fifteen-years-old.

William Price was also a southern sympathizer and worked for the Confederate army. On October 16th, 1861, Union soldiers knocked on the Price's front door and led him out of their house, down the road and questioned the man.

He never returned. They shot and killed him. The incident fueled Nancy's desire to find ways to help in the war effort. But she was not going to be seen sitting around sewing clothing for the soldiers or twisting her hands at the window waiting to hear the outcome of every battle.

Not long after the war began, she became a scout and spy for the Confederate Moccasin Rangers, a pro-Confederate guerrilla group led by a man named Perry Conley. In 1861, Union troops captured her, and she was able to convince them she was innocent and she was released. In July of 1862, she was arrested again in Summersville and deceived a soldier into letting her see his gun, which she used to murder him and escape. Nancy returned with 200 Confederate troops, leading them to the place where the skirmish to capture Summersville played out.

Nancy Hart.

A reporter with the Richmond Examiner described the battle as follows:

> "The gallant Maj. BAILEY, commanding four companies of cavalry -- in all about 150 men, sent to the rear of the enemy by Col. MCCAUSLAND --stormed Summersville, the county seat of Nicholas, Friday morning at daylight, and killed and captured the entire garrison, including the Lieutenant-Colonel commanding, named STARR, three other commissioned officers, and sixty-two non-commissioned and privates -- killing a large number. A few prisoners were paroled. Not being able to bring away the large quantities of Commissary, Quartermaster and ordnance stores found at the place, Maj. BAILEY committed them to the flames. Maj. B. brought to this place a large number of Enfield rifles and mules. The prisoners arrived this morning at the Salt Sulphur Springs." *LYNCHBURGH,* **Wednesday, July 30th, 1862.** *Correspondence of the Richmond Examiner.*

Nancy Hart would live to marry Joshua Douglas, a Moccasin Ranger. She also survived for 60 years. One of the Yankee boys who battled against the soldiers she followed to Summersville was not so lucky. A young Union soldier, whose dog always remained by his side, was mortally wounded. As he and a band of other soldiers retreated into the dusky edges of the evening, he began to grow too weak. The other men had no choice but to abandon him. The dog, however, would not leave his side. They both died there in the very spot the soldiers left them along Peters Creek. On warm summer evenings, when the wind whistles through the trees and past the little houses dotting the countryside, the low sound of a dog whining and the sorrowful moans of the soldier make their way to ears willing to hear them. Then, they fade away.

The roadway paralleling Peters Creek, where the ghostly sounds of a soldier's moans and a dog's sad whines ride the breeze on warm summer nights.

Henry Young's Grave
Youngs Monument Road
Birch River, WV 26610
38.44765, -80.79120

Young's Monument
38.463283, -80.782849

Nicholas County

The Headless Ghost Rider of Powell Mountain

A lonely tomb sits in the mountains near Birch River with a ghostly legend held in its grasp.

In the days before the September 10th, 1861 Battle of Carnifex Ferry, Union troops led by General Rosecrans were preparing to engage Confederates led by General Floyd on the Henry Patterson Farm, which overlooked Carnifex Ferry. Their movements toward the battlefield led them in a southerly direction near Birch River on Powell Mountain.

On September 8th, Confederates sent 34-year-old Henry Young and four other local militia and citizens to scout out the number of men in Rosecrans's forces. They came to the road, and Young was just a bit ahead when he saw Federal troops following his path. Knowing the rest of his small militia group were going to be overtaken, he stepped out from behind a tree and began to fire at the Union soldiers, sacrificing himself so the others could hear the shots and know to escape. He was shot in the head and cheek and died on the mountain. Fearing an ambush, his comrades could not retrieve Young's body for five days. A cousin returned alone, and buried the body where it lay. The road leading to the gravesite of Henry Young is graveled and lonely.

It is from the mountain gravesite and along the road where ghostly Henry Young rides. Most see him as headless, the close-range blast of the rifle left little remaining of his skull. He rides on a horse only to disappear at the bottom of the hill in a burst of light.

Henry Young's grave.

The haunted road.

A story was given to me from a woman whose great-grandmother, along with her father, saw the headless apparition of Henry Young and his horse as they drove past one day in the early 1900s. It appeared as if he was a human riding fast down the road until they realized he had no head. Then the ghost, in a ball-like blast of light, vanished. The event frightened the two and the horse so greatly, none could move. It was told and retold again in her family—then passed along to me.

Soule United Methodist Church and Cemetery
279 Farmdale Road
Western, WV 24958
37.921599, -80.696590
(Grave of Zona Shue)

Greenbrier County

Greenbrier Ghost —Jailed By A Spirit

A sign in Greenbrier County just off the highway on Exit 156 at Sam Black Church, (37.901852, -80.632401) tells a ghost story.

He had a handsome exterior, the mysterious man with brown hair, piercing blue eyes, and a powerful build who came to work for James Crookshank at his blacksmith shop in Livesay's Mill, a small town five and a half miles from Lewisburg. Those in town knew very little about the man.

Zona Heaster. Image: Greenbrier Historical Society Archives.

But some would admit that something just was *not right* about him. His past must not have mattered to 22-year-old Zona Heaster, a chestnut-haired beauty, and daughter of Mary Jane Heaster. He was quite the catch for a small-town girl, and there was but a brief courtship. The two married at the Old Methodist Church in Livesay Mill on October 20th, 1896.

But there were more than a few indiscretions overlooked by neglecting to dig into his past. Trout was from Droop Mountain in Pocahontas County. He had been married twice before. He wed his first wife, 18-year-old Allie Esteline Cutlip, on December 24th, 1885. The two had a child named Gertrude by February of 1887. Trout would divulge to some that his ex-wife was not a fit mother and the grandparents were raising his daughter. However, the truth was quite different. In reality, Allie complained his beatings were quite severe—he was said to have thrashed his young bride so badly, a group of vigilantes marched to his home on Rock Camp Run in temperatures below zero and tossed him in the frozen Greenbrier River. She was able to convince the courts of Edward's cruel nature and Allie would divorce him while he was in prison for stealing horses.

On June 23rd of 1894, 32-year-old Trout had married his second wife, 16-year-old Lucy Ann Tritt from Alderson and the two lived on Droop Mountain with his family. The circumstances were quite scheming on Trout's part. He had whisked the girl off and out of sight of her parents and talked her into marrying him outside county lines.

However, he did not have the proper paperwork. He then asked a minister to perform the ceremony who denied him, stating the girl was underage. Undaunted, the couple scurried to Frankfort and were married the next morning. Less than eight months later on February 11th, 1895, Lucy was dead at seventeen. She had died when she helped Trout fix a chimney in the cold months of winter. The man was perched on top and asked his young wife to get him a glass of water. When she returned, he dropped a brick on her head, crushing her skull.

If only Zona had known about his previous life, she probably would not have moved into a small two-story framed home owned by the town founder, William G. Livesay, which was on the opposite side of Sewell Mountain from Zona's mother.

Home where the couple lived in Livesay Mill.

Still, all seemed well for two months. Then Zona fell ill. She was treated by the family doctor, J.M. Knapp, and appeared to be feeling better within a few weeks. Then on a cold Saturday of January 22nd of 1897, Trout Shue went to the home of Martha Jones, fondly called Aunt Martha, to request her son, 11-year-old Andy, to do some chores including picking up eggs for Zona who was still recovering.

The boy was busy at the time and had some odd jobs to do for the local physician first. Trout returned four more times to collect the young man and each time, appeared more impatient.

It was late afternoon before Andy was able to get to the Shue home. When he walked toward the house, there was a certain air about the place that did not seem right, including someone had shut the doors tight. Upon closer inspection, the boy was shocked to find a trail of blood on the porch step. He knocked on the door and when there was no answer, Andy cautiously followed it into the house and through the dining room where he found the body of Zona lying at the bottom of the stairs leading to the second floor of the home. She was staring lifelessly at him with wide open eyes and lips parted. Zona was stretched out with feet together, one hand upon her abdomen, and the other lying next to her. Her head was turned slightly to one side. The boy mustered enough courage to shake her. When he did, she was hard and cold.

Shocked, the boy went to his mother who immediately fetched Doctor Knapp and Trout. But by the time the doctor made it to the home, Trout had already taken his dead wife to an upstairs room, laid her on a bed, and dressed her in different clothing. If the doctor found it strange, he did not make a note—it was customary for women in the community to redress the corpse. Trout had taken it upon himself to provide Zona with a high-necked stiff-collar and a crepe veil wrapped around it. But he appeared deep in grief, rocking his young bride back and forth holding her head. Quite possibly, it is the reason the doctor provided a clumsy attempt to examine the young woman and take into consideration the puddles of blood on the floor. He declared aloud: "It is an everlasting faint. Her heart has failed."

Doctor Knapp would report as his initial cause of death in the records in Lewisburg that Zona had died in childbirth.

> prox., at 9 a. m.
> Mrs. E. Z. Shue, wife of E. S. Shue, died at her home in the Richlands, this county, on Sunday last, the 24th inst., aged 22nd years. Mrs. Shue was a daughter of Mr. Hedges Heaster, of Meadow Bluff district. Mr. Shue formerly lived in Pocahontas county.

During the night and all through the wake, those family members and friends who surrounded the young woman's body noted that Trout hovered so strangely nearby his dead bride that they could hardly get close. On a chilly, rainy day in January, she was buried at the Soule Chapel Methodist Cemetery in Meadow Bluff. Trout was the last person to see his dead wife's face.

Local newspapers reported he took it upon himself to nail the wooden coffin shut before she was lowered seven feet deep into the West Virginia soil. A great many rumors began to spread throughout the small community that Zona's death may not have been by natural causes. Knowing something seemed fishy and being a spiritual woman, Mary Jane Heaster began to pray day after day for some truth to display itself and ease her grieving mind. Then, one evening, she heard a rustling in the room where she was praying, and before her appeared the very form of Zona. As the mother reached out to embrace the daughter, the ghostly form vanished.

Mary Jane Heaster, Zona's mother.

Now, knowing something was amiss, Mary Jane Heaster prayed once again, and her wildest fears would come true.

Her daughter would return, in the form as Mary Jane would describe as flesh and blood, and told her of the abuse the hands of Trout Shue had dealt her. On the night of her death, he had come home angry. In a fit of rage, because no meat was on the table, Trout broke her neck. To show the savagery, the otherworldly Zona turned her head completely around!

Mary Jane compelled authorities to exhume the grave of her daughter. Doctor Knapp (who had initially given her cause of death as childbirth), a surgeon by the name of Rupert, and Doctor McChesney performed the autopsy. On her throat, there were the marks of fingers indicating someone had choked her, and her windpipe was smashed.

Trout was arrested and taken to jail at Lewisburg. During the court battle, Trout's dark past began to bubble up. The peculiar man began to ramble and brag in his jail cell that there was no way anyone had enough evidence to convict him, and he intended to marry seven women. Yet, courts *did* convict Trout of first-degree murder. He spent the remaining years of his life in jail, dying during an epidemic passing through the West Virginia State Penitentiary in Moundsville on March 13th, 1900. Some will only recall Zona Heaster Shue as a poor woman who was murdered by her evil husband. But most will remember her as the Greenbrier Ghost—a young woman appearing after death to her grieving mother and, by doing so, helped convict an evil man of murder and, thus, avenge her death.

Zona's headstone. She still walks among the graves at the little Soule United Methodist Church and Cemetery.

John Wesley United Methodist Church
208 Foster Street
Lewisburg, WV 24901
37.799924, -80.444474

Greenbrier County

A Church with Much Spirit

John Wesley United Methodist Church.

The John Wesley Methodist Church in Lewisburg was built in 1820. It has a long history of the living passing through its doors. It also has a few who have lingered long after death. The spirit of a little girl killed on Foster Street bounces a ball outside the building where a stairway once stood by the sanctuary. The *thump-thump-thumpety-thump* sound of the ball can be heard by those passing by.

There is also the ghostly presence of a Confederate soldier. On May 23rd, 1862, the Battle of Lewisburg was in full swing. At five o'clock in the morning, Confederate soldiers firing guns and preparing for battle awakened townspeople. The battle lasted only twenty-seven minutes, but in that time, eighty Confederate soldiers were dead, and the Union took many as prisoners. The Federal army only suffered thirteen dead. The church became a makeshift hospital for the wounded, and it appears at least one man has never left. A young soldier lay injured near the church and died before being found. His spirit still remains along the outside walls leaving passerby with a feeling of sadness and loss.

Historic General Lewis Inn
1236 E Washington Street
Lewisburg, WV 24901
37.796560, -80.436022

Greenbrier County

Lady in White

Historic General Lewis Inn

Built in 1834 by the John Withrow family as a home for their son, this stately structure now houses a 25 room inn—and a few ghosts. A Lady in White haunts room 208, and the spirit of a little girl is seen at the end of the bed in room 202, startling more than a few guests.

Greenbrier Resort
300 W Main Street
White Sulphur Springs, WV 24986
37.785957, -80.308167

Greenbrier County

Ghosts Who Crave Luxury—Even after Death

People have been coming to White Sulphur Springs to rejuvenate since the late 1700s. The resort has accommodated 26 presidents, countless celebrities, and even professional football teams. It has ten lobbies, 20 dining venues, and 710 rooms—and golf courses. With such a rich history of visitation and a tendency toward the well-appointed, it is not surprising it has a few ghosts who like to stick around. A ghostly girl plays in the resort's parking lot, her giggles wafting softly in the air.

Kate's Mountain Road
Caldwell, WV 24925
37.763818, -80.301596

Greenbrier County

Kate's Mountain Bobbing Lights

Kate's Mountain.

In 1750, 36-year-old Nicholas Carpenter built a cabin near what is now Springhouse Lane within Greenbrier Resort. It was not the safest place to live; native Indians of the area frequented the springs, and by the mid-1750s, raids in the region were increasing. At this time, Nicholas decided to move his family to a safer location—Fort Young in Covington, Virginia, about 23 miles away.

Whether Nicholas left to help local militia fend off Indian attacks or if he was simply on the way to the stockade is uncertain. But during a raid along the Jackson River near Covington on September 14th, 1756, Nicholas was one of nine men attacked and killed. The Indians also captured three women and fourteen children. Many legends have arisen from this attack, including those that retell the ghost of Kate, Nicholas's wife, was among those killed. Her ghost haunts the mountain, such because of this event, the mountain bears her name. However, 31-year-old Kate, and Nicholas's youngest daughter, 11-year-old Frances, escaped by hiding at the nearby mountain peak and eventually made it to the fort safely. In 1784, Kate Carpenter sold the land where the cabin once stood at the springs. Captain Michael Bowyer, who also married her daughter, Frances, later developed the property into White Sulphur Springs resort. In honor of Kate Carpenter's daring escape, the mountain is called Kate's Mountain.

But there is a ghost that haunts Kate's Mountain.

Old dirt roads of Kate's Mountain where a legend came to pass.

Witnesses have observed strange bobbing lights halfway up the mountain and along the roadway, followed by a deep humming sound. Not long after, a ghost appears and stands with its head awkwardly bent at an angle. Some recall that it is the spirit of a wealthy baker who worked at the resort in the early 1920s and overly worried about paying his taxes. He walked partway up the mountain, then chose a tall tree. He placed one end of a window cord on a tree limb and the other around his neck. Then he hung himself.

Droop Mountain Battlefield
683 Droop Park Road
Hillsboro, WV 24946
38.114817, -80.269400
The museum and graves are located directly behind the park office.

Pocahontas County

Dead Horses and Headless Soldiers on Droop Mountain

Droop Mountain Battlefield.

On November 6th, 1863, the Union army advanced towards Salem, Virginia on a planned raid to disrupt the Virginia & Tennessee Railroad. They were waylaid by Confederate troops that had marched a grueling 27 miles on what is now US-219 to attempt to stop their assault.

The Confederate army was outnumbered, but held the high ground, blocking the highway so the Union could not advance. However, in the afternoon, the Confederate troops were overrun. It was considered a Confederate defeat. Still, the men stopped the Union troops from taking over the railroad. The fight lasted a day, much of it in hand to hand combat. The number of men who were killed or succumbed to wounds varies. At least 45 Union and 33 Confederate soldiers died. Since the clash, people have reported hearing sounds of a battle and seeing soldiers' spirits and a lone, misty horse. The pound of galloping horses echoes across the grounds and at least one person has seen a Confederate soldier settling in for a nap against a tree.

Lookout Tower for a full view of the ghostly area.

In the 1920s, Edgar Walton was one of two workers too tired to return home late one evening after logging at Droop Mountain. Instead, they decided to build a small fire and camp. Walton heard the leaves rustling and expected to see a deer foraging in the patches of grass beneath the trees.

Instead, he came face to face with the headless ghost of a Confederate soldier floating straight towards him. Just within reach, it turned toward a gate, disappearing. His story took place near the cemetery in what is now Droop Mountain Battlefield State Park.

The cemetery where a headless ghost of a Confederate solider has been seen is by the park office.

Suzanne Stewart, a staff writer for The Pocahontas Times, covered a story of the restless ghosts at Droop Mountain, interviewing former employees of the park and found an interesting account. It seems Napoleon "Nap" Holbrook was a superintendent for Droop Mountain Battlefield, Holly River State Park, and Tomlinson Run until he retired in 1981. When his son Alan was young, the boy would help his dad out at the park, picking up garbage and cleaning up around the picnic areas. One day while he was out with his dad, the two drove back to the house for a few minutes, and while Nap ran inside, Alan played with a little toy truck, quietly and intently focusing on rolling it around the door and the handle.

As he was playing, he heard horses outside the vehicle, tromping on the ground, snorting, and making a fuss. He thought it strange, the sound of galloping. When he looked up, there was nothing there. Then, just as he started to tend to his little toy again, he could hear horse hooves clomping up right next to the truck. Alan looked up, horrified. He distinctly heard a horse snort loudly, felt the tepid spray of slobber hit his cheeks while the breath blew back his hair. Nothing was there. Alan's screams brought the family quickly to the truck. It would be half a week before he would come outside without crying, and for years the ghostly memory of that moment lingered in his mind.

Some have heard the ghostly pound of long-dead horses here. I have visited the park many times, and each time I catch the scent of horses. It is enough to attract my attention as I have horses myself. I expect to look up and see one pawing the ground in front of me. Then the scent vanishes, and I question whether I smelled it at all.

Southwestern West Virginia

Camden Park
5000 Waverly Road
Huntington, WV 25704
38.397708, -82.531654

Cabell County

The Mound

Camden Park was developed in 1902 by the Camden Interstate Railway Company as a cozy picnic area for rail-weary train travelers heading through Huntington. Over the years, it changed hands and amusement park rides were included, from roller coasters to log flumes. It has become a place where families make many fond memories. A unique feature is an ancient Adena burial mound located in the center that is the third-largest mound found in the state. Visitors to the park report feeling uneasy near the mound and a sensation of being watched.

The Office of Doctor Grimes
1125 20th Street
Huntington, WV 25703
38.414004, -82.420277

Cabell County

The Haunt of Lavina Wall

Lavina's old home.

Haunted by the spirit of 21-year-old Lavina Wall—slender and dark-haired, she died of gastroenteritis, most likely by the poisoned liquor given to her to ease the pain after a fall down the stairway at her mother's home on October 28th, 1929. Lavina's ghost has been seen in the doorway, looking up the stairway. Some speculate her father murdered her, and she is trying to divulge the truth.

Fifth Street
1852 5th Street Road
Huntington, WV 25701
38.397371, -82.449285 (top)
to
38.406182, -82.447223 (bridge)

Cabell County

Fifth Street Vanishing Hitchhiker

The top of Fifth Street hill where cab drivers pick up a rider and she vanishes before they get to the bottom.

In late October 1942, a Black and White Cab driver had just dropped his customer off at a dance hall around 4:30 in the morning. He headed back to Huntington and had just topped the Fifth Street Hill, a roadway leading south out of Huntington and situated on a steep incline.

As the road leveled beneath his tires, a young woman hailed him from the side of the road. He stopped, opened the door for her, and noted quite quickly that she was not wearing a coat or hat, only a plain white dress. Teasing, he asked her why she was not dressed more warmly, and she answered: "I haven't worn a coat for nine or ten years."

The young woman asked him to take her the half-mile drive to the bottom of the hill. Driving only about 20 miles an hour down the hillside, the cab driver stopped at the bottom. He turned to ask for the fare and let the girl out of the car when he noticed she was not sitting in the back seat. He thought she might have fainted and fallen on to the floor, so he got out to make a thorough check of the vehicle. The cab driver was astounded she had completely vanished. He would report this: "—so I drove back to the taxi headquarters. I said to the dispatcher, 'I've just been gypped out of a quarter,' and I told him what had happened. He said he had heard of that same thing happening to a Yellow Cab driver about a year before in the same place and called up the Yellow Cab office and asked them about it. They said it happened to one of their drivers."

Over the years, quite a few drivers have picked up the vanishing ghost, including Greyhound and Trailways bus services. Those who hear her story have nicknamed the rider, *Ghost Girl of Fifth Street*. Most explain the mysterious hitchhiker as this: A couple was heading to Huntington to be married. The bride-to-be was wearing a simple wedding dress. Along the way, the driver sped off the road and wrecked the car, and the young woman was killed.

Frederick Hotel
940 4th Avenue
Huntington, WV 25701
38.421503, -82.441811

Cabell County

Spirited Reflections of a Bootlegging Past

Frederick Hotel

The grand hotel opened in 1906 with much fanfare and stayed open until 1973. It had such guests as Bob Hope and Richard Nixon. Diners have heard the sounds of children laughing and giggling in the restaurant area, and there are also reports of screams and footsteps and whispering. Rumors persist that the building was part of an underground tunnel system for bootlegging during prohibition. The ghostly sounds heard there reflect the criminal activities going on during that time.

**Greater Huntington
Cinema Theatre
(Keith Albee)**
1021 4th Avenue
Huntington, WV 25701
38.420783, -82.442908

Cabell County

Lady in Red and the Shadow-Man

Keith Albee.

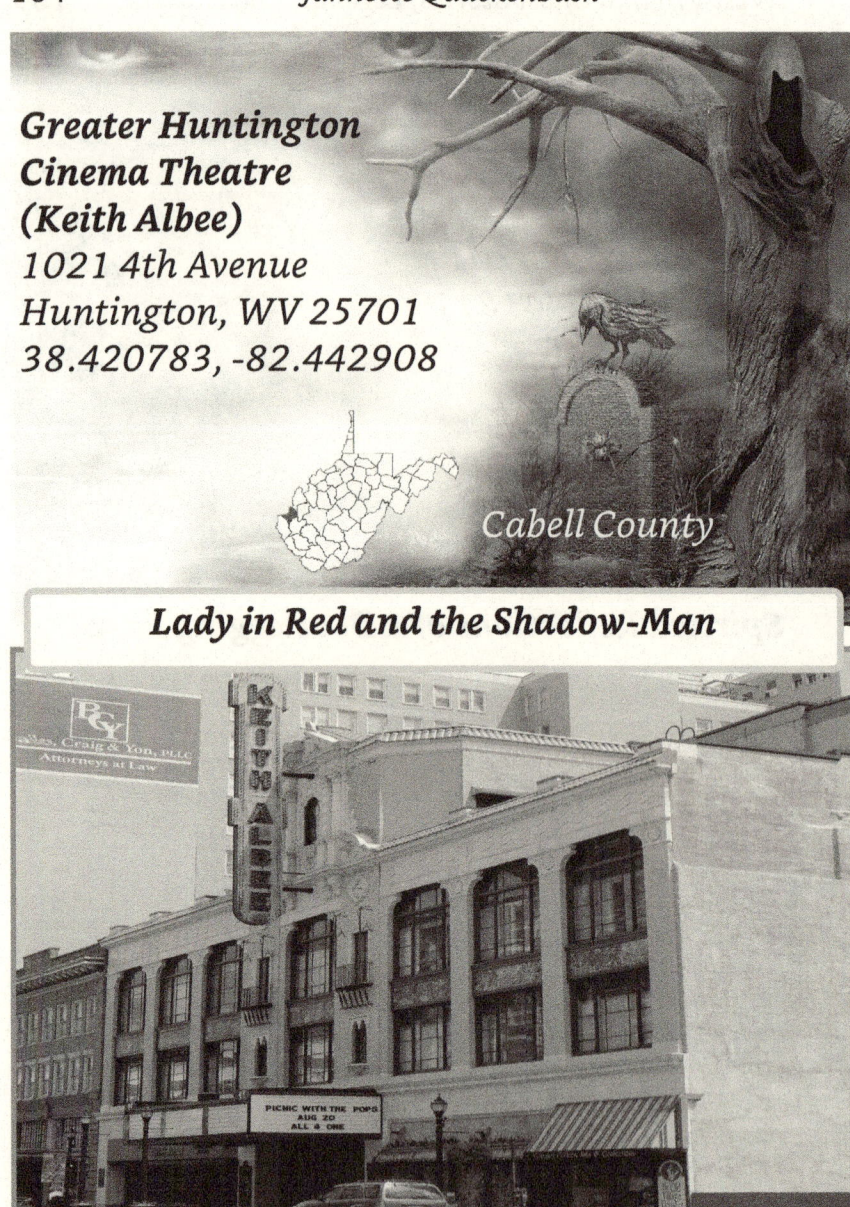

The Keith Albee Theatre was named for the Keith Albee Orpheum Corporation, a leading vaudeville performance circuit in 1928. A 1940s ghost in a fancy dress, *Lady in Red*, haunts the parlor near the restroom, most likely a visitor from its glorious past in vaudeville. A shadow-man is found where a maintenance man died in the projection room.

Spring Hill Cemetery
1427 Norway Avenue
Huntington, WV 25705
38.411473, -82.416601

Cabell County

Still Walking the Graves

Spring Hill Cemetery.

In 1874 when the city established Spring Hill, the price of a grave space was less than $2.00. It has such local notables as Dan Hill, Huntington's first cab driver. In the 1890s, Dan used a horse-drawn wagon to transport people around town. Seven members of the Marshall University Football Team, who were killed landing in a plane at Huntington's Tristate Airport, are buried at the memorial site located at the cemetery's 20th Street entrance. Among those haunting this city of the dead is an old caretaker for the cemetery that wanders the property, always watching to make sure someone is carefully tending to the graves.

Woodmere Cemetery
2701 Washington Boulevard
Huntington, WV 25705
38.405650, -82.399156

Cabell County

Mother Blood

While perusing the internet, I found an old legend about Edith Blood's grave, called *Mother Blood*. Edith died in 1939, but the stone has gained attention as one that glows and bleeds during nights with a full moon. Theresa Racer, the author of *Haunted Huntington*, has a great explanation for the blood—"The reddish stains dripping down the back of the stone," she states, "can be attributed to the natural weathering process and leaching of the stone, and possibly even stains from where a clip-on flower vase was positioned atop the grave. In fact, several nearby graves also have similar stains."

Bridge and Short Streets
Huntington, WV 25702
38.429163, -82.384424

Cabell County

Ghostly Woman in Black

The corner of Bridge and Short streets where a woman in black taunted walkers.

Guyandotte was a small but bustling port town along the Ohio and Guyandotte rivers in the 1800s eventually absorbed into Huntington. Along the way, though, the city had its share of bumps and bruises. In November of 1861, about 700 Confederates overcame about 100 Union recruits in a camp at Guyandotte. As the Confederates were withdrawing, Union troops came and burned part of the town in retaliation for the townspeople aiding their foe.

The town also had a ghostly *Woman in Black*. The Huntington Advertiser, on September 23rd, 1905, reported that a woman dressed in the darkest of blacks, a mourning dress, would frequent North Bridge and Short streets. She would keep pace with people walking the streets and stop whenever they stopped.

Guyandotte Cemetery
244 Guyan Street
Huntington, WV 25702
38.42833, -82.39000

Cabell County

Wandering Ghost of Eleonore LeTulle

Eleonore LeTulle walks from her grave to the gate at the far end of the cemetery.

Eleonore LeTulle died at the age of 73 in 1836. Her husband, Victor, buried her in the quiet Guyandotte Cemetery just a few blocks from their home and grocery business. He remarried not long after to Nancy Forgey, and the two raised their many children. When Victor died in 1853 from pneumonia, his family buried him beside his first wife, Eleonore.

When Nancy passed away in 1892, the family buried her in Spring Hill Cemetery. Nancy's children disinterred Victor and reburied him near Nancy. It was not taken well by the poor Eleonore left alone in the cemetery for eternity. She walks from her grave and to the cemetery gate and pauses before she makes her way up the street to her old home.

Hawks Nest State Park Overlook
17839 Midland Trail
Ansted, WV 25812
38.122805, -81.127798

Fayette County

Legends of Lover's Leap

The drop is 585 feet below the craggy cliff overlooking the New River Gorge. It has two legends born over time explaining how it got its unusual name—

Lewis Spring, now Lewisburg, was about 50 miles away from the area of Hawks Nest. Early surveyors found a large spring there, which enticed settlers into the area. It was not long before cabins began popping up in the region. In 1763, the native Indians destroyed the town, murdered the men, and kidnapped the women and children.

In 1770, the government created Fort Savannah to build a militia and stand against the Indians. Although the earlier pioneers fled during the French and Indian War, by the 1780s, they had returned to settle the area. It is here the story of two ill-fated lovers begins and ends. A young man and woman fell in love at this early settlement, and the girl's parents did not approve of her choice. The boy was from a very poor but respectable family who lived on a small farm, eking out little from their meager patch of land. Defying her mother and father, the young lovers ran off searching for a new settlement and a new life. When they beheld the magnificent cliff above the New River, they held hands and chose it as their place to live. Just as their fingers released, the girl felt dizzy and slipped forward. Before her lover could rescue her, she toppled over the cliff and fell to the rocks below. So distraught with grief, the young man leaped over the overhang, following her to his death below.

Lovers Leap in earlier years.

The parents left no time to search out the young runaway couple. They, too, paused at the cliff edge to take in the grandeur. One of them saw a cedar on the precipice edge and noted that a limb had been slightly split. With stunned realization, eyes slipped down the cliff to see the bodies of the two young lovers. It was with great sorrow they found the two dead along the craggy cliff, bruised and mangled but lying side by side. In despair, they would call it Lover's Leap, and forever, the rise would keep this name.

VIEW FROM LOVER'S LEAP, NEW RIVER CANYON, HAWKS NEST, W. VA.

Long ago, an Indian called Tame Eagle lived along the banks of the New River. He could blend the rushing sound of the water with the sweet melody of his flute. He fell in love with Amonita, the daughter of a neighboring tribe's chief who lived near a cliff across the river. She loved him too. Amonita would sit beside Tame Eagle singing songs with her sweet voice to the tune of his flute atop the cliff. But the chief did not condone their love. He decided to end their trysts, sending braves from his tribe to hunt Tame Eagle down. The couple heard them coming. There was no escape on the cliff. They clasped hands and jumped to their death.

Now, some days those near the river's edge hear the sound of Tame Eagle's flute in the rushing waters of New River. And Amonita's voice slides up from the gorge along with it, a reminder of two young lovers together for eternity.

Lovers Leap and along the trail where a ghostly white horse trods.

The best view of Lovers Leap is by taking the aerial tramway from Hawks Nest Lodge to the marina at the bottom of the New River Gorge and then taking a jet boat ride with Captain Rick and Sue.

Although it is most famous for its star-crossed lovers, the ghosts of suicides are said to haunt this cliff edge. Even in the early 1900s, the cliff has been a hotspot for falls and suicides. The ghosts of those who have made their last walk to the edge haunt the area around it. Ghostly yells and screams are heard in the darkness below the cliff. Some have seen a mysterious white horse coming up the treacherous trail along the mountainside!

Tracks Heading To the Ghost Town of Vanetta
Vanetta, West Virginia
38.175427, -81.193754

Fayette County

Ghostly Lantern in Vanetta

The haunted tracks in Vanetta.

Lynchburg Colliery Company opened the Vanetta mine in 1904 and soon after, a settlement sprang up just across the Gauley River from the Town of Gauley Bridge. There were not any roads to Vanetta. Those living there had to follow the Central Railway tracks or traverse a swinging bridge running across the river.

There were typically about 100 residents in the town, about 45 women, 43 men, and an odd assortment of children living in 41 shacks described as nothing more than hovels. Those in town suffered greatly. If it was not by poverty, it was with sickness. After the coal mines closed in 1927, the desperate, unemployed miners would find work digging the Hawk's Nest Tunnel and end up with lung disease from exposure to silica dust within the stone.

Tracks leading into Vanetta.

There have been the typical kinds of deaths associated with coal and rail towns, including George Dietz, who ran the coal company in the 1930s. Dietz was known to walk the tracks quite often like most who lived along the rails, smoking his cigars, which he dropped on the ground partially smoked. Everyone in town knew not to pick up his half-smoked stogies—one puff and you would be fired from the mines because Dietz would snatch them back up on his return trip and finish them by the time he got home. But in July of 1931, and at 58 years of age, Dietz would no longer be puffing his cigars along the old rail line. He was heading toward the Gauley Bridge along the tracks from Vanetta, and a train struck and killed him.

Dietz was not the only one to stroll along the railway. When I stopped at the gas station across from the Vanetta railroad tracks, a local told me a story passed down to him by his family who lived near the town. A ghost used to walk the tracks, and folks were scared to take the railway at night for fear of seeing a phantom lantern light hovering above the rails.

A woman living in the town of Vanetta would go down to the tracks and hang out with the hobos while her husband was working in the mines. He told her he better not find her down there, but the woman would not listen. The miner tramped down the hill and shot her dead one night. However, her ghostly form still walks along the abandoned stretch of banged-up rails to hang with the hobos each night. With a lantern bobbing in hand, she works her way along the overgrown path that was once a busy track near the town.

The abandoned set of tracks where the ghostly woman carrying a lantern is seen.

Railroad Tracks over Paint Creek
Pax, WV 25904
37.906968, -81.263658

Fayette County

Fayette County Lights

Train tracks by Pax where a ghost is seen.

For years, folks have witnessed lights along the train tracks between Weirwood and Pax. When followed to the bridge over Paint Creek, they eventually take form as a man who was killed trying to outrun a train years ago. Someone walking the tracks discovered his mangled body sprawled by a pile of derelict rail ties workers cast aside when old was replaced with the new, but his head rolled into the creek below, and no one ever found it. The headless man stumbles about and still searches for what he lost.

Glen Ferris Inn
9022 Midland Trail
Glen Ferris, WV 25090
38.150292, -81.214745

Fayette County

An Inn's Ghostly Guest

Glen Ferris Inn's ghost walks the floors.

Glen Ferris Inn is a historic hotel nestled on the Kanawha River banks and overlooking Kanawha Falls in the town of Glen Ferris. In the 1800s, it was used as a stagecoach stop and, during the Civil War, as a Union quartermaster's depot. The inn's ghostly past comes from the 1860s and with the appearance of a full-bearded Confederate officer called "The Colonel." The mysterious apparition is seen only from the waist up, and yet the sound of his footsteps are heard thumping on the floor. He has also startled unwary bystanders by slamming doors.

22 Mine Road
Holden, WV 25625
Entrance to Road and Drive:
37.796211, -82.107372
37.783812, -82.102540
Take the winding drive to the top of the mountain.

Logan County

The Secret Life of Mamie Thurman

The top of Trace Mountain, 22 Mine Road where Mamie Thurman's body was dumped and her ghost still lingers.

Mamie Thurman, ghost.

Garland Davis, a 32-year-old deaf-mute, was picking berries near the top of Trace Mountain near his brother's home where he resided when he stumbled across the grisly sight—the body of a young woman mutilated and huddled in a ditch. It was 2:00 p.m. Wednesday, June 22nd, 1932, a damp day with dew still clinging to the briers and scrubby berry leaflets on the mountainside following early morning rain.

The dark-haired woman's body was tucked into the brush approximately fifteen feet from 22 Mine Road, named such as it began at the base of Trace Mountain and ran to the No. 22 mines of the Island Creek Coal Company. The coal company was not in operation at the time, and the area was isolated. It was the perfect place for berry picking. It was also the ideal place to dump a dead body.

The state police were at the scene within an hour and identified the body as 31-year-old Mamie Thurman, a local housewife and the wife of Logan city policeman, 48-year-old Jack Thurman. Jack had worked as a municipal employee for just over a year. Mamie was well-known in the small community of Logan. She had left her job at the local bank recently to become a full-time housewife. She was taking a summer course at a local college, West Virginia Wesleyan College. Mamie was also an active church-goer at Nighbert Memorial in downtown Logan and a member of the Logan Women's Club.

Harry Robertson.

The couple rented a two-room apartment over a garage located in 42-year-old Harry Robertson's backyard. Robertson was the stereotypical version of a business geek with thick glasses, greasy hair, and starched suit, the bookkeeper at the National Bank of Logan, and a prominent figure in the city. He was also an avid sportsman. Mamie had also worked alongside Harry Robertson at the National Bank and golfed regularly with Robertson's wife, Louise.

The authorities accessed the scene. Mamie was wearing a blue cotton dress with white polka dots. The dye of her dress had faded onto her undergarments, suggesting she had been lying on the patch of land during the heavy thunderstorm occurring just a few hours earlier. Two doctors confirmed that she had been dead for approximately twelve hours.

Their theory was that someone had murdered Mamie Thurman elsewhere, and her body was disposed of on the hillside sometime during Wednesday morning at a remote dumpsite known to locals. She was wearing one shoe, and searchers could not find the other. Those on the scene had Mamie's body transported to the funeral home for autopsy.

The Justice of the Peace and acting coroner, L.V. Hatfield stated on the death certificate: *Manner of Injury: Pistol shot and knife. Nature of Injury: 2 bullets fired in brain & throat cut.* It was an understatement. The autopsy report specified her throat was slashed—the cut on her throat had severed the trachea, jugular vein, and ceratoid artery. There were two .38 caliber pistol bullet holes on the left side of her head that had passed entirely through her skull. One came in behind her left ear and exited above her right. The second penetrated above the left and emerged at the top, rear of her head. The police did not find either bullet. Mamie's neck was broken, she had bruises over her right eye, and gunpowder burns on her face. Police discovered a kitchen knife 150 feet from her body, wet with blood, and her hat about 30 feet away. R.B. Harris, the local undertaker, could not pinpoint if she had been stabbed or shot first.

Clarence Stephenson.

Nothing at the scene suggested robbery was the motive. Her pocketbook was near her body and contained eight dollars in cash, loose change, and cigarettes wrapped in paper. She was wearing a wristwatch, a gold diamond ring, and an engagement ring. The police began questioning neighbors and friends. Quickly several names came up leading to two suspects—that of Harry Robertson and then the handyman who boarded in the attic of Robertson's home, 29-year-old Clarence Stephenson.

State police searched Robertson's house during the funeral and as the whispers were circling the town. They found a depression on the basement wall that was suspect of a bullet hole, bloodstains on both the carpet and a razor, and blood on the seat and window of the Ford Sedan Robertson owned.

Harry Robertson, the couple's landlord, and his black handyman/chauffeur/hunting chum, Clarence Stephenson, were accused of the murder. Robertson readily admitted to having an affair with Mamie for nearly two years. Clarence Stephenson arranged the meetings, feigning hunting trips with Harry Robertson, then dropped his accomplice off at certain rendezvous points to meet Mamie.

The Grand Jury never indicted Harry Robertson. Stephenson continually stated he was innocent and witnesses could account for his whereabouts during the time of the murder, even when the man was taken up to 22 Mine Road and threatened to be given over to KKK if he did not confess. Still, Stephenson was indicted and stood trial for the death of Mamie Thurman. He was found guilty and sent to Moundsville Prison on August 22nd, 1934, and eventually died at Huttonsville Prison in April 1942.

And Mamie's ghost haunts the mountain road where her murderer dumped her corpse. She is seen at the top of the mountain, walking along the roadway. Crashing in the woods and footsteps are often heard by those driving near the top of the hill. Some witnesses report screams followed by gunshots. Along the old road, coal truckers have stopped to pick up a dark-haired woman in a cotton dress and provided her a ride, only to find her seat vacant at the bottom of the mountain. Even on the four-lane highway, US -119, drivers have reported a woman wearing a white dress ambling along the roadway near the 22 Mine Road sign.

Many believe Mamie is looking for the person who actually murdered her because the one sent to prison was not her killer. She will not rest until courts bring her real murderer to justice. But that is not all. Legends in the area recall that vehicles parked at the bottom of 22 Mine Road and placed in neutral will roll uphill. It is Mamie's ghostly hands pushing the vehicle. More than a few have witnessed the event. They divulged to me that if you put baby powder on the bumper of your car, you will have proof—her delicate handprints will be left in the powdery residue.

So, will your car move? Yes. After a couple of locals swore to me that it would work, I tried it several times at the stop sign at the bottom of 22 Mine Road. I placed my jeep in neutral (with someone watching for traffic coming along the twisting turn of 22 Mine Road because vehicles do come down the incline), and the jeep backed up a minimum of ten or twelve feet on its own. Is it an optical illusion, a mystery hill phenomenon, made by the layout of the land? Maybe. But I still like to think it is a ghost.

Me in my jeep actually trying out the legend (I had helpers watching for traffic) and yes, the vehicle moved!

Hatfield and McCoy Country

Mingo and Logan County, WV & Pike County, KY

The Spiritual Remains of Feuding Families— Hatfields and McCoys

So, about those Hatfields and McCoys and the few ghosts that hang around their story—

In all reality, they would be just two families living opposite each other on the Tug Fork of the Big Sandy River with homes scattered up and down the small creeks in the valleys if it were not for the feud. The Randolph McCoy family lived mostly on the Pike County, Kentucky side. The family owned a 300-acre farm and livestock and dealt in illegal moonshine. Almost all the McCoys residing in the area fought for the Confederacy in the Civil War, except Asa Harmon McCoy (1828-1865), who was a younger brother of Randolph and who fought for the Union.

Randolph "Randall" or "Ole Ran'l" McCoy (1825-1914)

On the other side—the William Anderson "Devil Anse" Hatfield family was mainly from Mingo County, West Virginia. The Hatfields had a pretty successful timbering business and employed more than a dozen men, sold illegal moonshine, and fought on the Confederate side.

They were both prominent families in a rural area and hardly much different than any other families struggling in the late 1800s during a Civil War and standing on the cusp of a coal mining revolution.

William Anderson "Devil Anse" Hatfield (1839-1921)

That is, until 37-year-old Asa Harmon McCoy mustered out of Company E, 45th Regiment of the Kentucky Infantry for the Union side with a broken leg on December 24th of 1864. He reenlisted but was sent home on leave to mend his wounds. He came home to a chilly welcome from his southern sympathizing family and a warning from the Logan Wildcats, Confederate Home Guards, that told him they were going to visit him. Devil Anse Hatfield created this particular company of about 85 militia men to help in patrolling and protecting the valley around the Tug Fork during the war.

Asa Harmon McCoy (1828-1865)

Only thirteen days after Asa Harmon had returned home and only a few months before the end of the Civil War, he had gone out to take water from a nearby well. Hearing gunshots, he found refuge in a cave along Blue Spring Creek.

His slave, Pete, brought him food. He was still wounded and suffering from lung fever. It did not take long for one of the Logan Wildcats to find Pete's tracks in the snow. He followed the steps to the cave where Asa Harmon McCoy was hiding.

On January 7th, 1865, Asa Harmon was shot and killed. James Vance, a tall and heavyset uncle of Devil Anse Hatfield and a member of the Logan Wildcats, was the suspected killer. Authorities issued no warrants for the murder, and his wife's sworn statement after his death was: *killed by rebels while returning to his regiment*. But there was a bit of a grudge that began to fester like an open wound between the two families.

Site of Asa Harmon McCoy's murder about 7 miles from Matewan:
Big Blue Springs Road
Ransom, KY 41558
37.557625, -82.191690

Relations became more rancid as the years went on, including land disputes in the 1870s. Violence would erupt again in the autumn of 1878 when Randolph McCoy was visiting relatives and happed upon a valuable hog in the field of Floyd Hatfield, a cousin of Devil Anse, that appeared to have the notched ear markings of his hogs.

Known as the Hog Trial Cabin, this replica of the original building was Preacher Anderson "Anse" Hatfield's cabin along Blackberry Creek. He presided over the dispute between Floyd Hatfield and Randolph McCoy over the hog. This cabin and surrounding lot was also the hub of community events such as local elections. If you visit, take a look at the top steps leading to the cabin. You'll see two little footprints in the concrete, remnants placed there by two of Preacher Anse's young grandkids.
Hog Trial Site
KY-319, McCarr, KY 41544
37.580175, -82.179955

Randolph accused Floyd of penning up the hog, and Floyd denied the claim. They brought it to Preacher Anderson "Anse" Hatfield's attention, and he presided over the dispute at his cabin. A relative of both parties, Bill Staton, affirmed it was Floyd's hog. Not long after, in a fight with Sam and Paris McCoy, Bill Staton was killed. His two killers were acquitted.

Amidst this drama, there was a bit of romance and betrayal in the story to fuel the feud's fire. It would occur in the same locale as the Hog Trial Cabin, along Blackberry Creek at a local election gathering in 1880 when 22-year-old Roseanna McCoy (Randolph McCoy's daughter) stumbled upon 19-year-old Johnson "Johnse" Hatfield (Devil Anse Hatfield's son).

*Roseanna McCoy
(1859-1889)*

*Johnson "Johnse" Hatfield
(1862-1922)*

Johnse was already a notorious bootlegger and known lady's man. Roseanna and Johnse slipped away for a few hours, and when they returned, almost everyone had left for the day, including Roseanna's brother, who had taken her to the event. Fearing the reaction of her parents, Roseanna McCoy rode home with Johnse Hatfield to his family home.

The two hit it off quite well for a while, and despite the romance was forbidden by both sides of the family, it continued, and Roseanna became pregnant with Johnse's child. Roseanna moved in with the Hatfields for a short time on the promise Johnse would marry her. Still, Johnse was seeing other girls, including her young cousin. When Randolph McCoy learned of the affair, he had refused to speak to his wayward daughter. Knowing a marriage would be doomed regardless, even the Hatfields would not support the relationship going further. Such it soured. Discouraged, Roseanna left to live with her Aunt Betty McCoy along the Tug Fork.

Still, Johnse continued to visit Roseanna off and on, and it angered her brothers greatly. Acting as deputies and in retaliation, they planned to have Johnse Hatfield arrested for old warrants. They apprehended him and took off for the Pike County jail. For the safety of Johnse, Roseanna made a midnight ride to warn Devil Anse Hatfield of the plans, which eventually led to Johnse's safe return home. Despite her bravery, Johnse left Roseanna to marry her cousin, 15-year-old Nancy McCoy. Her father would not forgive her for turning her back on the family, and she never returned home. Roseanna and Johnse's baby, Sarah Elizabeth (Little Sally), died with measles before she was a year old. The ill-fated Roseanna lived to be 30 years of age.

The grave of Roseanna's baby, Sarah Elizabeth (Little Sally): She was born in spring of 1881 and died of the measles at 8 months of age. She is buried beneath a cedar tree. The cemetery was a family cemetery located above Betty and Uriah McCoy's house, Roseanna's aunt and uncle in Kentucky, where Roseanna lived after leaving Johnse Hatfield.

Roseanna's Baby's Gravesite
Lower Stringtown Road
Goody, KY 41514
(37.630016, -82.220574)

The feud continued to gain force. Probably the most horrible incident was yet to come on Election Day—August 7th, 1882, when a fight broke out on the election grounds along Blackberry Creek in Kentucky between 29-year-old Tolbert McCoy (Randolph's son) and 39-year-old Ellison Hatfield (Devil Anse's brother).

The Hatfields around 1897.

Two of Tolbert's younger brothers Pharmer—age 19, and Randolph Jr.—age 18 rushed in to help. Randolph Jr. stabbed Ellison Hatfield with a small pocket knife he had in his pocket. Pharmer snatched up a pistol and shot Ellison in the back just before he hit Tolbert in the head with a stone.

Ellison Hatfield was taken down the Blackberry Creek to see a doctor. Meanwhile, the McCoys ran to the woods. Later, the men were apprehended by Kentucky lawmen, the Hatfields, and placed into the custody of the justice of the peace. However, the McCoy brothers were intercepted and seized by Wall Hatfield and Elias Hatfield convincing the lawmen to turn the three over to them for a "civil trial" at Blackberry Creek. The young men were escorted across the Tug Fork to West Virginia, away from the law. At this point, Ellison was still alive. Sarah McCoy pleaded for her sons' release. Devil Anse said that if Ellison lived, he would bring the three men back to Kentucky alive. On August 9th, 1882, news was released that Ellison had died from his wounds.

The three young men were taken to a pawpaw grove, tied to trees, and shot to death. The event would be known as the Paw Paw Tree Incident.

The area of the Paw Paw Tree Incident in Buskirk, Ky near the town of Matewan. Tolbert, Pharmer and Randolph McCoy Jr were captured and brought here and tied to pawpaw trees. The Hatfields fired over 50 shots into the McCoy men for killing Ellison Hatfield. The paw paw trees no longer remain. However, spirits might. The ghosts of the men are said to visit the section of land. Voices and mumbling have been heard.
2-198 River Street
McCarr, KY 41544
37.618716, -82.165350

In 1886, a couple of Hatfields went across the river to Kentucky and beat Mary McCoy Daniels and her 16-year-old daughter, Victoria. Her 27-year-old brother, Jeff McCoy, tried to chase the Hatfields down. Twenty-two-year-old Cap Hatfield and Tom Wallace killed Jeff McCoy on the Tug Fork banks. The governor called for the arrest of the murderers and placed a bounty on the men's heads.

It came to a head on New Year's night of 1888. The Hatfields ambushed the Randolph McCoy home and lit it on fire to flush the family out. A two-hour battle ensued. Randolph escaped into the woods with his toddler grandson. Twenty-six-year-old Calvin, Randolph's son, was shot and killed. Thirty-year-old Alifair McCoy, crippled by polio, tried to get water from a pump to extinguish the fire. She was unarmed but shot dead. Her mother, running to the woman's side, was beaten badly.

All that remains of the home site after the fateful fire and shootings that killed Alifair and Calvin McCoy is a hand dug well (center) that Randolph McCoy and his family used to draw water. Just beyond is the area where the homestead once stood.

*4087 US Hwy.
319 Hardy, KY 4153
(37.603132, -82.215412)*

And are there ghosts at the old homestead? I asked Neal Warren that question. Neal lives not a stone's throw away from where the old McCoy cabin stood and loves to greet guests visiting the grounds, giving them all the interesting and little known facts about the site. He told me he is not much of a believer, although he respects those who are not as skeptic. Still, he divulged that he was quite surprised when a gentleman with a ghost box (modified radio that scans radio frequencies for communicating with the dead) stopped in one day and asked to walk the property.

Neil Warren, left. Sam Quackenbush, right. Homestead and well are beyond.
If you're lucky when you visit the old McCoy Homestead, you'll get to meet Neil Warren, who lives next door to the site where the homestead stood and loves to greet tourists coming to the site. He may be out there to greet you with fascinating information you never knew about both the Hatfields and McCoys because he knows descendants from both sides.

The ghost box reacted with a few sayings that could not quite be coincidental. At the grassy area where the old McCoy homestead was burned to the ground by the Hatfields, there were three words stated: *blood, hot, and fire.*

West Virginia Ghost Stories, Legends, and Haunts 195

Near the area where Randall McCoy corralled his oxen and horses, the ghost box repeated: *animals, coup!*

Across from my son, you may be able to see the ghostly form of a woman in a long dress and bonnet holding something in her hands. When I pulled up the image on my computer, I asked my son if he had seen her because he is looking right at the object she is holding in her hands as if she is telling him something about it. He said "I turned because I thought I heard someone say something behind me—"

On January 18th, 1888, Kentucky authorities rounded up nine of the murderers in what was to be called The Battle of Grapevine Creek. Special officer Frank Phillips came in with the posse. The Hatfields were fully armed and waiting.

Area of Battle of Grapevine Creek
4897 WV-49
Matewan, WV 25678
37.579480, -82.123663

They clashed at Grapevine Creek, killing two of the Hatfield gang. They rounded up the rest of the Hatfields, and they spent years in court. When it was all said and done, eight of the killers were found guilty and sentenced to life imprisonment. The only one executed, the ninth, was the mentally disabled son of Ellison Hatfield, Ellison Mounts or "Cotton Top," who pleaded guilty, then tried to change his plea. On February 18th, 1890, officials hanged him in Kentucky's last execution. His last words were: "They made me do it. The Hatfields made me do it."

Cotton Top

Hanging of 26-year-old Ellison (Hatfield) Mounts — "Cotton Top". The image and explanation below was provided by G-man (Find a Grave). Ellison is kneeling, third from the right, with his head bowed. Fearing retribution, two men standing on the left side of the scaffold covered their faces with their hats, and the second kneeling man on the left obscured his face with his hand so they could not be identified.

*The site of the hanging today.
196 Kentucky Avenue
Pikeville, KY 41501
37.479558, -82.521711*

Devil Anse had 14 offspring. That's Tennyson 'Tennis' Hatfield (1890-1953) on the left hand side, front. He was Devil Anse's youngest boy. Neal Warren got this little ditty from Hatfield descendants about Tennis who was seven years old in the picture and he told it to my nine year-old son— Notice the pout on the little guy's face. He is not too happy compared to the image in the previous family photo taken the same day. It seems Tennis wanted to hold one of the guns for the photo shoot like Coleman Hatfield (1889-1970— Cap Hatfield's son who was Devil Anse's second eldest son) in the previous picture who was in the second row, far right. His daddy would not let him. He must have taken insult that the other boy was permitted. Especially because Coleman would have been Tennis's nephew and only a year older than him!

I heard once that one of the Hatfield girls wrote "There is no place like home" on a white pillow sitting on a chair on the family's front porch. Someone in passing, a stranger no less, added this in ink beneath, "At least this side of hell." Eventually, the feuding would rot away in the same way a raccoon left dead on the highway disperses to the wind. Randolph and Sarah McCoy moved to Pikeville. Randolph died on March 28th, 1914. Many of the McCoys, including Roseanna, Randolph, and Sarah McCoy, are buried in the Dils Family Cemetery in Pikeville, Kentucky.

*Graves of Sarah and Randolph McCoy, right.
To left, Roseanna's grave.
Dils Cemetery
104 Chloe Creek Road
Pikeville, KY 41501
37.477690, -82.515279*

Anse Hatfield spent his last years quietly on his farm. In 1911, he was baptized by old friend, "Uncle Dyke" Garrett, who was also the famous preacher who spent his life riding his old mule up and down the mountains to visit the sick and to preach to those who would listen.

Grave of Devil Anse Hatfield

Hatfield Cemetery
12560 Jerry W Highway
Sarah Ann, WV 25644
(37.704234, -81.992206)

On January 6th, 1921, at age 82, Hatfield died from pneumonia and was buried in the Hatfield Cemetery outside the town of Sarah Ann. The ghosts of Anse Hatfield and his sons remain. They return on foggy nights— rising from the graves. They make a quiet march down the mountain and toward the small Island Creek at the bottom. When they reach the creek, Preacher Garrett rises and baptizes them, washing away all their sins. Then, they disappear.

Hatfield Tunnel
1382-2144 River Road
McCarr, KY 41544
37.627200, -82.181871

Pike County, KY

Hatfield Tunnel Creeping Crawler

The Hatfield Tunnel is still in use. I cannot stress enough that unless you want to end up a ghost, too, stay away from the tracks.

The expansion of the Norfolk and Western Railway in the late 1800s included many parts of Southern West Virginia with the main focus of getting to the rich coal found here. The entire line was finished on November 12th, 1892, with the completion of the Hatfield Tunnel just outside Matewan.

Passersby have seen a ghostly form near the tunnel's entrance crawling on all fours between the rails still used by trains. No one knows who it could be—a miner who died digging through its core or a trainman killed in a wreck. This tunnel is no stranger to deaths—during the construction of the tunnel, miners died. There is little more than a small cemetery to mark their existence at all on the steep mountainside. The tunnel had its usual deaths, like locals cutting through it—in 1904, 27-year-old Elias Hatfield, freshly pardoned from jail and newly married to a coal-operator's daughter was killed walking within.

During 1901, floods swept through West Virginia, and the tunnel became a trap for the bodies piling up along the Tug Fork. That year, the water rose so quickly at one point, they found a dead horse and a dead rider with his feet still stuck in the stirrups!

> .. The region from Ennis to Davy, forty-three miles, is completely in ruins. Hundreds of mine mules can be seen in heaps intermingled with human bodies. A report has reached here that fifteen bodies are lodged in a drift at Hatfield tunnel, twenty miles east of this here. **Marietta Daily Leader., June 27th, 1901**

And then, there was the train wreck:

> The Norfolk and Western railroad is still clinging to the old saying that wrecks come in threes. Less than ten days ago there was a dead end collision at Hatfield tunnel in Mingo county which brought instant death to two engineers and two firemen. **The Big Sandy News., December 18th, 1903**

The tunnel is no stranger to death—it is almost like a magnet drawing people into its grasp and perhaps spitting them back out as ghosts. If you hap across the tracks while wandering the Hatfield-McCoy territory, watch out for the trains still bustling through the tunnels at great speeds. But also, keep a wary gaze out for the dead, well, a ghost. It might get you too.

The Grave of Octavia Hatcher
Cemetery Road
Pikeville, KY 41501
37.481080, -82.520137

Pike County, KY

Octavia Hatcher—Buried Alive

The grave of Octavia Hatcher with son's grave in front. She is missing a hand that once held a parasol and large ring.

Twenty-year-old Octavia Hatcher died on a warm May 2nd day in 1891. Or so they thought. Married in 1889 to James Hatcher, she had given birth to their first child, Jacob, on January 4th of that same year. Jacob died within hours of being born and Octavia was distraught over his death. As the months passed, her pain seemed to deepen and she became weaker. She fell ill and went into a coma and died. The young woman was buried quickly in the local cemetery to avoid spread of disease.

Within a few days, others in the community began to have the same coma-like symptoms—but they eventually awakened. Octavia's loving husband, James, felt a horrible realization overcome him. Perhaps his wife had been in a coma too! Cemetery caretakers immediately exhumed the young woman's body. When workers opened the casket, it was a ghastly sight—Octavia had not died at all. She had ripped the top of the coffin to shreds, her fingernails were bloodied, and her face was contorted in terror.

The family reburied Octavia, and her husband built her a new monument above her grave. Over the years, people have reported hearing mewling sounds near the grave. An apparition of Octavia walks through the cemetery, and during certain times of the year, her statue will completely turn so that her back is to the town that ignored the fact she was buried alive.

Octavia Hatcher's grave is in a quiet cemetery above the town of Pikeville, Kentucky. I found this legend when working on the Hatfield-McCoy feud ghosts. It was so close to them and so unique, I figured if you were already visiting the area, you would not want to miss this one!

The Ghosts of Matewan

Matewan Massacre
Area of Shootout
Hatfield Street
Matewan, WV
37.623112, -82.165258

Mingo County

Ghosts of Matewan-
Where to Look For Hauntings

Matewan in its early days and the place where ghosts stories are made—a bloody battle occurred right here between miners and a private detective agency, Baldwin-Felts, working for a coal company.

Matewan has ghosts. It should. It is home to a bloody battle where coal miners were pitted against coal companies ending in 10 lying dead in the streets in only a few minutes.

On a hot summer day when I stood in the spot where a battle played out, I could almost hear the shouts of the men, the blast of guns firing, and the *ting* of bullets ricocheting off brick walls.Some say the ghosts of Matewan's past lingering on the streets will never leave even though their voices in life were, eventually, heard. But it is all about the drive for rights, for what is due that leaves these spirits hanging around. And the men who left their mark in history in Matewan will forever be walking the streets in spectral form to remind others they did not die in vain—

Early West Virginia coal miners. Image: Library of Congress.

Matewan was founded in 1895 along the Tug Fork of the Big Sandy River, which separates West Virginia and Kentucky. It was among many towns in West Virginia that mining, coal, and timber companies had converged upon to obtain the rich resources. When the coal company came to Matewan, it ran just about every aspect of the coal miner's life—they built homes for the workers, schools, churches, and recreational facilities. The company owners sold from their stores, and miners were paid with company scrip that could only be redeemed at the company store. Mining was dirty and dangerous work, but it provided a living.

The town was independent of the Stone Mountain Coal Corporation who ran the coal and mining in the area. Matewan had only a few elected officials, including Sid Hatfield, the police chief, and Cabell Testerman, the mayor. Between 1919 and 1920, a strike by the United Mine Workers resulted in wage increases to coal miners in parts of the U.S. Workers in West Virginia would not benefit from this because they had yet to organize a union. However, the thought of earning higher wages piqued the interest of those miners in Mingo County, including those working for the Stone Mountain Coal Corporation in Matewan.

In 1920, over 3000 miners working in and around Matewan signed Union cards. In retribution, the coal company hired Baldwin-Felts Detective Agents, a private security force, to evict the miners and families from their homes. At 11:47 a.m. on May 19th, 1920, the battle would begin. Baldwin-Felts Detective Agency set foot on Matewan soil and began to evict a dozen miners and their families from company-owned homes.

The evictions, themselves, were peaceful. Chief Hatfield led the men to the homes and oversaw the process. After a late afternoon meal, about 4:00 p.m., at Urias Hotel, the Baldwin-Felts workers made their way to the train depot to head back to the company headquarters in Bluefield. Chief Hatfield and Mayor Testerman requested a meeting with Albert Felts in Chambers Hardware Store, challenging the agent's ability to evict within city limits as it was unauthorized by law. But as an exchange began, both men started to arrest the other. The men drew their guns, and Felts and Mayor Testerman fell wounded. Eight more men—six agents and two innocent bystanders—lay dead on the streets between the depot and town in minutes.

> **DETECTIVES AND MINERS IN BATTLE.**
>
> *Ten men were killed in a pitched battle at Matewan, Mingo county, late Wednesday afternoon, between members of a private detective agency and miners formerly employed by the Stone Mountain Coal Company at Matewan, who are reported to have been evicted from company houses by the officers.*
>
> *In the absence of Gov Cornwell, Col. Jackson Arnold of the department of public safety took charge of the situation and ordered his entire force to Matewan. Company B. from Nitro, was the first to reach the scene Thursday morning, the telephone reports late Wednesday night said all was quiet and no further trouble was anticipated. The dead are seven members of the Baldwin-Felts Detective Agency of Bluefield, two miners, and Mayor Gabell Testamen, of Matewan. Five others are reported wounded.* **Greenbrier Independent., May 21st, 1920**

The state police were called in and ended the violence for the moment. Murder charges were brought against Chief Hatfield and 17 strikers, but all were eventually acquitted. A year later, Baldwin Felts agents gunned down Chief Hatfield and his deputy, Ed Chambers, on the McDowell County Courthouse steps in Welch.

West Virginia Ghost Stories, Legends, and Haunts 209

Where to look for ghosts: The gunfight occurred in the area between the building and along the railroad tracks on Hatfield Street—

The street and tracks where the gunfight played out.

Keith Gibson, Hatfield and McCoy Boat Tours, shows the bullet marks left on a wall after the Matewan Massacre.

West Virginia Mine Wars Museum
336 Mate Street
Matewan, WV 25678
37.622765, -82.164903

For more information on the mine wars. It is located in the old Chambers Hardware. The building was once owned by the father of Sid Hatfield, deputy sheriff. Here, Hatfield planned the ambush of the Baldwin Felts guards coming to catch the train.

Grave of Smilin' Sid Hatfield
Buskirk Cemetery
Bowling Road
McCarr, KY 41544
37.618441, -82.168468

Pike County, Ky

Buskirk Cemetery—Smilin' Sid Hatfield Still Looking for Justice

The grave of Matewan police chief, Sid Hatfield. His ghost has been seen walking the cemetery.

Downtown Matewan is not the only place that has ghosts from the coal mining battles. If you do not know where they are, you can ask Joe Vagott, whom I found sitting at the front desk at the Matewan Depot Welcome Center. Joe is the resident ghost storyteller and offers ghost walks in town.

He told me Buskirk Cemetery, just a stone's throw across the Tug Fork and in Pike County, Kentucky, is haunted by none other than Chief Sid Hatfield. Smilin' Sid, as he was called because of his signature grin, was the small but wiry, 30-year-old chief of police who was a large part of the Matewan Massacre and whose murder would fuel the great Battle of Blair Mountain in the late summer and early fall of 1921. In a nutshell, the Battle of Blair Mountain was the largest labor uprising in the United States where miners were pitted against coal mine operators using strikebreakers and lawmen as their shield to stop unionization. But enough said. Here is the story-

Joe Vagott—resident story-teller.

Now, Smilin' Sid Hatfield did not die in the gunfight at Matewan. A few weeks later, he married Mayor Testerman's widow, Jessie. Although some folks alleged Sid Hatfield had shot Cabell Testerman to marry Jessie, it was never warranted nor proven. The two men had been close, and Testerman asked Hatfield to watch over his wife if anything happened to him. But in an unrelated trial in August of 1921, Sid Hatfield and his deputy, 22-year-old Edward Chambers, accompanied by their wives, were climbing the steps of the Welch Courthouse when Baldwin-Felts agents gunned down the men in cold blood in retribution for the Matewan shootout.

Sid Hatfield. Photo courtesy: e-WV: The West Virginia Encyclopedia

Sid died with three wounds to his chest. An agent finished off Ed Chambers with a shot to his head. In the end, the courts charged the killers with murder, yet they were never convicted of the crimes.

The grave of Sid Hatfield. The grave states: "To the memory of Sid Hatfield, May 15, 1893—Aug. 1, 1921. Defender of the rights of working people. Gunned down by Felts detectives on the steps of the McDowell County courthouse in Welch, W. Va. During the great Mine Wars. We will never forget. His murder triggered the miners' rebellion at the battle of Blair Mountain."

It is the perfect potion for a ghost story—the murder of a man who upheld the justice in his community and whose own killers were never brought to justice. It should not be surprising that a man with such spirit and clinging to that injustice would return after death to walk the cemetery where family thought they laid him to rest. And Smilin' Sid Hatfield does just that in the Buskirk Cemetery. He walks the cemetery near his grave.

West Virginia Ghost Stories, Legends, and Haunts 213

More Places to Visit and Discover Ghosts in Matewan:

Hatfield and McCoy Airboat Tours
Bridge Street
Matewan, WV 25678
37.622692, -82.168379
Exhilarating ride down the Tug Fork with local, Keith Gibson, giving the lowdown of ghost stories, myths and legends of the area.

Old Hospital—Matewan Clinic
Main Street
Matewan, WV 25678
37.622833, -82.166697—
This building was used as a hospital/clinic.

Historic Matewan B & B
155 Mate Street
Matewan, WV 25678
37.622904, -82.165817—
This cozy bed and breakfast was once used as a funeral home.

Matewan Depot and Welcome Center
328 WV-49
Matewan, WV 25678
37.622699, -82.168722
Historical displays and ghost walks.

Dingess Tunnel
County Highway 3/05
Old N W Railroad Bed Road
Dingess, WV 25671
37.864547, -82.180138

Mingo County

Thrilling Ghostly Ride in Dingess Tunnel

In the 1890s, Dingess was a lumber boomtown and trading center. It was also the nearest rail point on a new branch of the Norfolk and Western Railway, the Twelvepole Creek route—where, along this track, workers built a 3,327-foot tunnel.

Later abandoned, the railway and the tunnel became part of the highway, now cars can traverse through the interior. If you do go, watch out for ghosts in this dark passage christened America's Bloodiest Tunnel. Several tragic freight train wrecks occurred within, and it once had a dark history of violence for outsiders coming to work in the area. Many are known to have been brutally murdered there in the early days.

If you enter the tunnel, turn on your lights, indicating that you are entering to opposing traffic. There is only room for one car at a time.

Citations

Citations for Stories:
County Map: http://d-maps.com/m/america/usa/virginieoccidentale/virginieoccidentale/virginieoccidentale48.gif
Small county maps:David Benbennick - The maps use data from nationalatlas.gov

Cabell County:
Newman, Rich. Haunted Bridges: Over 300 of America's Creepiest Crossings
Platania, Joseph. Huntington Quarterly Magazine Ghost Stories
October 30, 1942 Herald Dispatch
Huntington Paranormal Investigations and Research (2006-2011). Keith Albee Theater. Retrieved May 3, 2011 from http://www.huntingtonparanormal.com/keith_albee_theater.htm
Wikipedia (2011). Keith Albee Theater. Retrieved May 3, 2011 from http://en.wikipedia.org/wiki/Keith-Albee_Theatre

Doddridge County:
Athens Messenger July 8, 1927. Ghost of Mountaineer Murdered Two Years Ago Said to Haunt Old Home.
The Sandusky Star Journal. July 8, 1927. Ghost Stories Heard Where Man was Murdered Some Years Ago.
http://www.doddridgecountyroots.com/tng/getperson.php?personID=I57629&tree=dcr

Greenbrier:
Shue Home: From http://www.prairieghosts.com/shue.html; should be public domain
www.appalachianhistory.net/2015/01/greenbrier-ghost.html

Jackson County:
Musick, Ruth Ann. Coffin Hollow and Other Ghost Tales University Press of Kentucky, 1977
http://wvncrails.weebly.com/bo-ripley-branch-millwood-to-ripley.html
The Headless Horseman of Donohue Lane. Jackson Herald March 29, 1940
Jackson County Map Archives
War Department Record of Pension
1940 Federal Census Jackson County
County Land Deeds –Jackson County
http://generations-past.net/donohue/headless-horseman.html
https://archive.org/stream/slaughterofpfost00morr/slaughterofpfost00morr_djvu.txt
Morrison, O.J. The slaughter of the Pfost-Greene family of Jackson county, W.Va. A history of the tragedy
The slaughter of the Pfost-Greene family of Jackson County, W. Va. : a ...
https://www.loc.gov/item/12026591/
Fort Wayne Weekly Gazette December 23, 1897

Jefferson County:
THE GILDER LEHRMAN INSTITUTE OF AMERICAN HISTORY- Letter Mahala Doyle to John Brown, November 20, 1859. (Gilder Lehrman Collection) - https://www.gilderlehrman.org/sites/default/files/inline-pdfs/T-07590.pdf
Velton, John J. The History and Operation of the Ferry formerly at Harpers Ferry.

Bluefield Daily Telegraph may 6, 1984
Dougherty, Shirley. A Ghostly Tour of Harpers Ferry. EIGMId Publishing. 2009 African American Trailblazers in Virginia History Dangerfield Newby's Letters from His Wife, Harriet Page 1 of 2 Publications and Educational Services Harriet Newby's letters to Dangerfield Newby, April – August 1859.
Governor's Message and Reports of the Public Officers of the State, of the Boards of Directors, and of the Visitors, Superintendents, and Other Agents of Public Instruction or Interests of Virginia (Richmond, 1859), 116- 117. Special Collections, Library of Virginia, Richmond, Virginia.
http://www.harpersferrywv.us/about.htm
Brennan, Patricia. HARPERS (HAUNTED) FERRY: SLAVE, PRIEST. https://www.washingtonpost.com/archive/lifestyle/1982/10/29/harpers-haunted-ferry-slave-priest-38/40939266-c36e-4a49-a152-a54da24f94f2/?utm_term=.919f1854749a
Brown, Stephen D. Ghosts of Harpers Ferry
https://www.dreamstime.com/royalty-free-stock-image-aerial-view-harpers-ferry-national-park-image20139806
http://www.harpersferrywv.us/about.htm
Brennan, Patricia. HARPERS (HAUNTED) FERRY: SLAVE, PRIEST. https://www.washingtonpost.com/archive/lifestyle/1982/10/29/harpers-haunted-ferry-slave-priest-38/40939266-c36e-4a49-a152-a54da24f94f2/?utm_term=.919f1854749a
Brown, Stephen D. Ghosts of Harpers Ferry
Gregory, Linda. Frederick News-Post. October 28,1985
Ashtabula Star Beacon October 22, 2001
On a Tour Of Harpers Ferry's Favorite Haunts: Spirits of Harpers Ferry Thomas, Dana The Washington Post (1974-Current file); Oct 31, 1989.
Costello, Michael A., Letter to Father Harrington, All Hallows College, February 11, 1860, Archives of the Roman Catholic Diocese of Richmond. Transcribed by Christopher C. Fennell
Historic Shepherdstown & Museum ; http://historicshepherdstown.com/2016/06/our-own-ghost-of-shepherdstown/
http://www.shepherd.edu/lib/shwebsite/legends/yellowhouse.html
http://www.shepherd.edu/lib/shwebsite/pdfs/yellowhouse/yellowhouse_legend_1928yearbook.pdf
Shepherd College Picket. October 28, 1954 Restless Spirit Roams College Campus Haunts Old High Street Cottage
The Wilmington daily Republican. (Wilmington, Del.), January 22, Shepherdstown register., June 17, 1892,
Brown, Stephen D. Ghosts of Harpers Ferry
Marmion, Annie P. Under Fire, An Experience in the Civil War

Logan County:
Beckley Post Herald June 25 1932. HEARING TODAY IN LOGAN CASE
Charleston Daily Mail jun 25 1932 Two Are Heard
Charleston Daily Mail October 11, 1932 Hearing Opened For Stephenson
http://www.onlyinyourstate.com/west-virginia/gravestones-wv/
https://www.geocaching.com
Pike County, Ky Travel and Visitors Bureau
The Wheeling Daily Intelligencer., January 27, 1888
The Memphis Appeal., February 18, 1888
Bluefield Daily Telegraph July 4, 1899
History.com The Hatfield & McCoy Feud
Donnelly, Shirley. Beckley Post-Herald August 7, 1957 Hatfield-McCoy Feud 75 Years Old Today

Mason County:
The Weekly Register. Pleasant, Mason County WV January 15 1896
The Point Pleasant register. (Point Pleasant, W. Va.), March 23, 1910, March 23, 1910

Mingo County:
Savage, Lon. Thunder in the Mountains. Pittsburgh: University of Pittsburgh Press, 1990.
The West Virginia Encyclopedia. Matewan Massacre
Greenbrier independent., July 16, 1920
The West Virginian., May 21, 1920
The Daily Ardmoreite., May 20, 1920
Gibson, Keith. Hatfield/McCoy Boat Tours

Nicholas County:
Sutton, John Dawson. History of Braxton County and Central West Virginia
http://theresashauntedhistoryofthetri-state.blogspot.com/2011/07/henry-young-rides-on.html
The WPA Guide to West Virginia: The Mountain State - By Federal Writers' Project
MacLean, Maggie. Nancy Hart Douglas. Confederate Spy and Guerrilla Fighter
Powell, Bob. Rebel Spy Nancy Hart Leads Raid at Summersville: July 25, 1862. Aug 2016
https://www.findagrave.com/cgi-bin/fg.cgi?page=gr&GSvcid=657559
www.wvdar.org/WilliamMorris/Morris%20Massacre.htm

Pike County:
Asa McCoy Union Soldier https://www.ancestry.com/mediaui-viewer/tree/113379655/person/350113435406/media/9d97d570-eeef-4922-8557-ca92a2a2e00e
https://www.findagrave.com/cgi-bin/fg.cgi?page=gr&GRid=3061
https://www.findagrave.com/cgi-bin/fg.cgi?page=gr&GRid=9401298
http://www.tourpikecounty.com/5-things-you-may-have-missed-at-the-hatfield-mccoy-feud-sites/
e-WV: The West Virginia Encyclopedia
Taxewell Republican—April 9, 1908

Pleasants County:
Ikie mooring. (n.d.). Retrieved from https://www.findagrave.com/memorial/120837817/ikie-mooring
Mt. Welcome cemetery, Pleasants County, WV. (n.d.). Retrieved from https://www.wvgenweb.org/pleasants/cemetery/mtwlcm.htm
Tice, John Goldenseal Magazine, Fall 2003: Searching for Ikie's Tomb.
West Virginia vital research records - Record image. (n.d.). Retrieved from https://www.wvculture.org/vrr/va_view.aspx?Id=4753871&Type=Death
https://www.gardenofinnocence.org/miranda-eve-childs-casket-found-under-home (Elissa Davey and Garden of Innocence provides burials for abandoned and unidentified children)

Pocahontas County:
Droop Mountain Battlefield State Park
www.droopmountainbattlefield.com/

The last sleep - Charleston Gazette -www.wvgazettemail.com/News/201311090049
The Battle of Droop Mountain https://www.mycivilwar.com/battles/631106b.html
Cincinnati Enquirer (1872-1922); May 28, 1881; After Eighteen Years—Description of the Battle of Droop Mountain, West Virginia
Porterfield, Mannix. Cumberland Evening Times October 28, 1985 Ghosts Come Out All Year 'Round in West Virginia.
Cumberland Times News. October 28, 1985.
Shepherdston:
Shepherdstown register., May 06, 1920, More About that Duel
Shepherdstown register., April 21, 1898. A Duel at Shepherdstown

Ritchie County:
National Railway Bulletin, Volume 59 Number 1, 1994
Summers County:
Greenbrier Ghost
Raleigh Register September 19, 1952. Bugs, Dust..Stafford, Thomas
Findagrave.com https://www.findagrave.com/cgi-bin/fg.cgi?page=pv&GRid=40813714&PIpi=153901390
https://en.wikipedia.org/wiki/List_of_counties_in_West_Virginia
Estaline Cutlip: https://www.ancestry.com/family-tree/person/tree/109703192/person/260078261748/facts
http://www.register-herald.com/news/did-testimony-come-from-beyond-the-grave/article_b1139217-3b58-5582-b652-a81149c551bb.html
Guiley, Rosemary Ellen. The Big Book of West Virginia Ghost Stories
The Big Book of Ghost Stories Series Publisher   Stackpole Books, 2014
Post Herald April 25 1973 Greenbrier Ghost Story Detail Added By SHIRLEY DONNELLY
Beckley Post Herald And Raleigh Register November 12, 1977 Ghost Solved Crime By SHIRLEY DONNELLY
Marion Sentinel October 14, 1897 Jailed by a Spirit
Post Herald March 5, 1953 Waking 'Em Up. Eugene L. Scott
Greenbrier Independent, February 25, 1897, Foul Play Suspected
Staunton Spectator and Vindicator., July 08, 1897 Trial of Trout Shue
Greenbrier Independent., July 01, 1897 Testimony of Mary Heaster. Mrs. Mary J Heaster, the Mother of Mrs Shue Sees Her Daughter in Visions
Greenbrier Independent., July 15, 1897 Lynching Foiled

Lewisburg
https://greenbrierhistorical.wordpress.com/2013/07/03/civil-war-in-greenbrier-county-the-battle-of-lewisburg/
Richmond, Nancy. Haunted Lewisburg West Virginia
Kate's Mountain
A centennial history of Alleghany County, Virginia [database on-line]. Provo, UT: Morton, Oren Frederic,. A centennial history of Alleghany County, Virginia. Dayton, Va.: J.K. Ruebush Co., 1923.
Resorts at the Mineral Springs. Greenbrier, West Virginia Pioneers and Their Homes
-The Wheeling daily register., September 01, 1877, Kate's Mountain
Washington County, MD
http://www.history.com/topics/american-civil-war/battle-of-antietam

Made in the USA
Monee, IL
24 November 2021